TANNERY BAY

TANNERY BAY

A NOVEL BY STEVEN DUNN AND
KATIE JEAN SHINKLE

TUSCALOOSA

FC2 is an imprint of the University of Alabama Press

Inquiries about reproducing material from this work should be addressed to the University of Alabama Press

Book Design: Publications Unit, Department of English, Illinois State University; Director: Steve Halle, Production Interns: Barry Taylor and Peyton Teague

Cover image: Jon Flobrant (@jonflobrant)/Unsplash

Cover design: Matthew Revert

Typeface: Adobe Jenson Pro

Library of Congress Cataloging-in-Publication Data is available from the Library of Congress.

ISBN: 978-1-57366-205-5

E-ISBN: 978-1-57366-907-8

Once upon a time people said some babies here are born with their heads too big or with too many of them, skin searing off and eating itself. The group of men who own everything in this town—the casino, the tannery, the old fishery, and the newspaper—say it's all good. Nobody's dying. Nobody has a baby with a head too big or born with too many of them. Everyone's skin is shiny, intact, and not slowly eating itself.

In the graveyard across the bay bridge from the dilapidated casino, Otis kicks a gravestone with his lanky, thin legs, and then takes off his browline glasses to clean with his shirt because he thinks the dark and shifting shadows are making him see a woman he's never seen before.

He remembers kicking a gravestone as a kid, he thinks, and his pops shaking him saying it was disrespectful. But they're dead now, how could they even know? "How could they?" he says aloud to the egg-rotten, pink-leather air forcing the trees to droop lower. The perfume factory, as it is locally known, makes everything stink in Tannery Bay, where purple chemicals pour out of four large pipes straight into the water, and heavy, white, hot smoke pumps incessantly from the stacks above.

Otis exits the graveyard, and starts the mile walk across the cracked and crumbling bridge. The purple bay water is calm for his entire walk, but he keeps taking his glasses off and putting them back on because he thinks he hears something splashing. Maybe it's them man-size rainbow trout the old fishermen always lying about, he thinks. Otis is on his way to work at the casino. Ahead the only indications of the casino's existence through the fog are two sad beacons of light shooting up to the sky until the heavy, white, hot smoke swallows them.

When he finally gets to the entrance with the fake, towering, gold arch, he thinks about turning around, no, not just turning around, but going in and standing on top of his blackjack table and pissing all over the tattered green felt, *then* turning around. No, not turning around yet, but slapping the fuck outta his boss *after* pissing on the blackjack table, then turning around and walking his happy ass back across the bridge, cutting through the graveyard, and back to his apartment on Bowfin Street to take a nap. A good nap.

He doesn't. He walks through the fake gold arch, through the main floor, and down the hall to the Floor Manager's office to clock in. When he clocks in for his second shift of the day, his boss, the Floor Manager, asks about the scuff on his left boot, always his left boot, every day, from walking through the graveyard and kicking a gravestone.

Otis tells him he kicked the curb before walking into the casino and drifts off into thought: Curbs are gravestones, too, because somebody probably lived here before this stupid casino was built. Ain't it disrespectful to kick a curb? Maybe with enough kicking of gravestones and curbs, it will rattle those old bones and those dead folks will snatch all the coin, take over the casino.

"Shine that shoe!" the Floor Manager says. "I want you pristine before you go out on the floor."

Otis takes himself out of his fantasy and says, "It could happen."

Then he signs his name on the daily log under July 37. Nobody knows the year, but tomorrow is July 2 again.

July 2

Once upon a time in the casino up the street from the tannery, Otis goes through the motions of dealing cards across the faded and ripped green felt of the blackjack table, trying to keep his mind from sinking into wherever it goes by focusing on the regulars in front of him. The woman enters the casino. Otis watches her jump from the highest point of the fake gold arch, walk through the clear doors without opening them, through the brass bellhop cart in the way of her path. A woman wearing tan waders and a white T-shirt, wet black hair hanging over her face.

The same woman Otis thinks he sees every night at the edge of the graveyard after he kicks a gravestone. She's never there before he kicks it, only afterward. Whatever, Otis thinks, I wish her weird-ass luck on the slots. The woman walks up to Otis's table and has a seat, even though there were no open seats available a moment ago. As soon as she sits, the other people at the table vanish. She moves her hair out of her face, and her eyes flash images of a baby walking on water. A baby who looks like his niece, Cora Mae. On the ripped felt, she projects an image of Otis's hand holding another hand, a hand Otis recognizes because of the small scars from needle points on the outer edge of the index finger. She mouths, "It could happen." The other people reappear. Someone yells "Hit me!" and taps his card against the table. Otis deals. The woman disappears.

Across the way, all the slots ring at once with no one at them, cherries and red sevens spinning until ding ding ding, cockle shells spill into the metal trays and onto the floor. No one pulled the levers. The three people at the table say "Deal another card, chief!" Otis deals but he's watching the woman. There she is again, leaning up against the end of the row of slots, hair over her face. The wails of the machines above everything makes the floaters in Otis's eyes dislodge; all he can see are dots scattering everywhere.

"Let me get a square," Otis says to the man in front of him.

The man knocks one out of the pack and asks, "When did you start smoking?"

Otis nods his head. The flame in thin air. The flame out of nowhere. Then, there is no one in front of Otis, a soft pack of Bay Pleasure Kings still wobbling on the seat.

"Ten-minute break!" his boss says. "Clean these cards up! Why hasn't anyone been at your table all day? Quit smearing ash on the felt!" Right outside the door, from the corner of his eye, Otis sees the sparkle inside of a cockle shell on the ground in front of the fake gold arch. He leaves his table, bends over, picks it up, and puts it in his pocket. The other cockle shells spilled out from the slot machines are gone.

He goes outside. His breath puffs light pink, and he huffs into his hands to warm them up. "It's freezing out here," he says. Everyone stops.

"It's hot as hell," someone says. "It's summertime!"

At the end of his break, he returns to his table. New people are seated across from him. People his boss keeps smiling at. He doesn't like the way his boss keeps smiling. He goes through the motions of dealing cards again, but he can't stop thinking about the woman in the waders. The cockle shell in his pocket feels hefty, so heavy it pulls down his pants and he has to keep tugging them back up throughout the rest of his shift.

Six-thirty a.m. The dirty pink sun never brightens the sky, only tints the thick white smoke blanket above. Smoke mixed with dirty pink makes a dirtier pink. Before walking out of the casino, Otis wraps a scarf around his neck once, then again around his neatly lined mustache and short beard, and pulls his red beanie down to cover the top of his ears. His twin sister, Joy, is getting off work from the tannery at the same time. Otis stands on the curb and watches her all bundled up walking in the middle of the street toward the casino, her big afro silhouetted by the dirty pink sun behind her. They hug, and Joy smells like animal hide and chemicals, slightly stronger than the air.

"How was work?" Otis says.

"Bad as always," Joy says. "Why you always ask the same shit?"

"Because, one day I hope the answer will be different."

"Well it ain't," Joy says. "How was work for you?"

"Bad as always."

They walk the mile back across the cracked and crumbling bridge in silence until they reach the graveyard carpeted by pink bay fog. Joy and Otis are both fumbling with their pockets, the cockle shells weight like cinder blocks. Otis rubs one between his forefinger and thumb. Joy holds one in the palm of her fist like a prayer.

Joy scans the edge of the graveyard, "This is where I've seent that weird-ass broad—I thought I recognized her."

"Weird-ass broad?" Otis says.

"Broad with waders on and stringy hair all in her face like a nasty," she says. "She came in the tannery and stared at me for a bit and kept getting closer to me, mouthin somethin. I ignored her for the longest. Boom, she was right in front of my vat! I couldn't ignore her anymore. I was like, "What are you sayin, nasty, speak up!" The woman's eyes flashed a baby walking on water, straight up looked like Cora Mae. I swear to god, when I tell you, she just poof! Vanished, gone, and all the hides in the soaking vats rose up in the air and stretched out, drippin everywhere, stainin everything. Then, they splashed back down. And guess what was right there on my workstation? Juice's tool belt . . . you know the one. He didn't even let me touch that thang. He had it on the night he died. We buried him in it. And now it's on my workstation. Everybody else act like they ain't seen shit. But, woo it got to my nerves."

Otis grips his cockle shell hard in his hand, tells Joy about what happened at the casino.

"Man, we should sit in the middle of this graveyard and wait for her. Tell her ass to leave us alone," Joy says.

They sit on the steps of the mausoleum, each of them not telling the other one about the cockle shells in their pockets. The morning pink gives way to purple fog. They wait and wait, each of them pointing out shadows, yelling for her to show herself. Each of them taking turns saying "What the fuck?" at every creak and groan of the otherwise silent graveyard. The woman in waders never arrives. They finally decide to head home to their apartment on Bowfin Street. As they walk out of the graveyard, Otis looks back to the mausoleum steps, and swears he sees two cockle shells right where they had been sitting.

"Whose birthday is it today, son?" Otis and Joy's neighbor, Willie Earl, yells from his balcony on the ground floor. He's already laughing and playing cards with Delores and her smooth fade with three lines on the side. Her shiny red bike is leaned against the railing. Otis doesn't know if Delores is on her way to work as a housekeeper in the Hills, or if she's gonna go hang out at the corner store with the rest of her butch crew who all slap their knees like old men when they laugh and smoke Bay Pleasure cigars, letting the thin and sweet plastic tips hang from the sides of their mouths. "I said whose birthday is today?" Willie Earl yells again.

Otis and Joy ignore him and walk up the three flights of stairs to their apartment. As soon as they open the door, there she is, the woman in the waders standing in the middle of their living room. Otis rubs his eyes, blinks hard. Joy says, "Not today!" The ay-ay-ay echoes out the door and back down through the stairwell. The woman is gone. The only evidence she had been there is wet bootprints in front of the door, fresh mud. Otis and Joy run back down the stairs until they're on the street.

Willie Earl is still slamming cards down, yelling to Delores, "You know how Anita got these sculptures beaming all over town, that's how I am with these cards, a goddamn AR-TEEST!"

Delores says, "You ain't shit, Willie Earl. I gotta go to work, anyway. I'll be back tonight, babe."

Willie Earl slams another card. "Them rich white folks up in them Hills will understand if you need to stay here a little longer to finish getting mollywhopped," he says.

Joy and Otis ask Willie Earl and Delores if either of them saw a woman in tan waders come out the building. Delores says she hasn't seen anything but Willie Earl's ass-kicking he put on her. Willie Earl says that's all he's seen, too.

Everything is the same as always: everyone holding tight to their beers wrapped in paper bags. The kids next door on their bikes, watching the teen boys play basketball in the middle of the street. The teen boys who use a plastic crate as a hoop. The girls with their half shirts and hot pants sitting in the grass watching them, braiding each other's hair, being loud. Charlene is sniffing around the girls, asking people if they got a light, asking people if they got a dollar, asking the girls which boy is their boyfriend, yelling at the boys to run faster, jump higher, because she wants to see the outlines of their dicks in their shorts.

"Keep it moving now! Stop fretting teenagers about their jelly rolls!" Willie Earl yells to Charlene, laughs a belly laugh that makes him cough.

The front door slams open by itself.

"You see her anywhere?" Joy says, as she taps Otis on the shoulder. He jumps.

"Yo, quit scarin me!" he says. They have been standing next to each other the whole time, and he didn't even notice the door. Here comes Uncle Gerald walking out of his house across the street, his big hands holding Joy's four-year-old daughter Cora Mae's tiny hands. Cora Mae's small afro puffs glistening with hair grease. She only has one head, but they joked she'd have three since both of her parents, Joy and her boyfriend Juice, worked at the Tannery.

Otis says "Heeeeey, baby!" and picks up Cora Mae when she and Uncle Gerald cross the street. He puts her on his shoulders. "Happy Birthday!"

Willie Earl yells again, "Happy Birthday Cora Mae! It's my birthday, too. And Charlene's! Ain't that right, baby."

Charlene says, "Sure is. These boys right here remind me of you, Willie Earl." She picks up the out-of-bounds basketball and throws to the boys.

"Shiiid," Willie Earl says, laughing. "You don't know nothin about me."

Willie Earl's laugh jumps the porch, launches over the lawn, dunks itself through the hoop.

Everyone, for as long as they all can remember, was born sometime between July 2nd and July 37th, so there are so many birthdays every day. They heard there used to be twelve months, so when you have twelve birthdays, that makes a year. This is Cora Mae's forty-eighth birthday, so she's four years old. Uncle Gerald might be around sixty or seventysomething. Auntie Anita might be around sixty or seventysomething, as is Willie Earl. They all lost track because they said it ain't important. Otis feels the same, but he cares about the kids' birthdays, because he hopes if they ever get out of July, they'll still be young enough to care about their ages. He hopes they're not jaded, and are able to look someone in the eyes and say, "Happy Birthday, I'm so glad you were born." Otis still looks his niece in the eyes and repeats his fantasy.

"Happy birthday, Cora Mae, I'm so glad you were born."

"Why?" she says, smiling.

"Because I love you."

"Why do you love me?"

"Because you're such a sweet and silly kid."

"Why am I such a sweet and silly kid?"

"Because you just are, now please stop asking me why because we'll be here all goddamn day."

Cora Mae starts running in circles saying, "All goddamn daaay," over and over. Uncle Gerald lifts her up onto his wide shoulders and joins her song. They all walk back across the street to Uncle Gerald and Auntie Anita's house, and head upstairs to the living room. There are muddy bootprints leading up the stairs and over to the dining room table. Auntie Anita is scrambling eggs and frying bacon, biscuits cooling on the stovetop, while patting the fresh haircut she always has: short curls swooped to the side and faded into the sides and back. She is singing a song about rapture she's been singing forever, but says she doesn't know where she got it from, it's inside of her. She turns from the stove and says, "Y'all see that stringy-ass woman who tracked mud in my house?" Auntie Anita didn't tell them that the woman in waders also left colorful mud on the kitchen floor. Blue mud made a sky with a yellow-mud sun spreading rays over a circle of people dancing.

"I ain't seen nobody," Uncle Gerald says.

"She's my friend!" Cora Mae says.

"We saw her, she tracked mud in our house, too," Otis says.

"Who the hell is she?" Auntie Anita says turning back to the stove and scraping eggs and bacon onto a platter.

"She's my friend!"

"We don't know," Joy says, "But that broad was at our jobs last night trying to scare people. Maybe Otis was scared, but you know good and goddamn well I wasn't."

"She's my friend, but she sure do scare mommy," Cora Mae says, mostly to Uncle Gerald, still on his shoulders. "You was too scared, Mommy!"

Auntie Anita walks over to the table, places the platter and the basket of biscuits in the center, and sits. She turns the corner of her mouth up and taps her foot while nodding her head: "She been in my dreams, but now she in the world. Hmmm . . . maybe something is coming, this feel different. We need to pay attention."

Uncle Gerald takes Cora Mae off his shoulders, and sits next to Auntie Anita, "You know I love you, Anita, but I can still recognize when you saying some crazy mess."

Auntie Anita stares at him over her glasses, and points the spatula at his chest: "Just because ya ol deep-voice ass say some shit you think is logical don't mean it's the authority—I know what I'm talking about. And that baby know what she talking about."

"You right," Uncle Gerald says. "It do feel different this time. I don't know what exactly feel different, but if you and Cora Mae say so, I'm with it."

"Alright, everybody get a plate, let's eat, no eggs are good cold," Auntie Anita says as she shoves a whole biscuit in her mouth without splitting it or smearing jam or butter on it.

July 3

Once upon a time in the graveyard next to the dilapidated casino, Gerald and Anita are walking home when Gerald scoops Anita around the waist and dips her and they start to tango, Anita's red shawl flowing in the wind around her. Gerald fumbles a bit with his footwork, the gravel underneath catching his shoes. No matter, he wants to keep up with Anita. Anita, who is a few half inches shorter than him in high heels, is quicker, far more graceful, light on her feet. Always has been.

Gerald was Anita's only boyfriend. Anita dated a woman named Rocko for as many Julys as she could remember. When she found herself attracted to Gerald, too, she knew her heart was big enough for both and that felt right. When Gerald was away, she was all Rocko's. When Gerald was back, she split her time between them. She loved Rocko, but knew Rocko wasn't the one. She loved Gerald, but knew Gerald wasn't the one.

Back in the day, Gerald used to get locked up on trumped-up charges because the Owners who wanted all the money in Tannery Bay were mad because everyone was going to Gerald's juke joint, gambling a little, drinking a little, dancing, eating a lot of fried fish sandwiches. This was before the casino, when the only place in town to gamble was Gerald's. The cops said Gerald was running a whorehouse, which wasn't true. As far as Gerald was concerned, folks met up at his place, but they waited until they got back to their own joints to juke as much as they wanted. They'd lock Gerald up for a July, then he'd get out and open the juke joint again. After a while, the town enacted a new ordinance declaring gambling illegal. Gerald was locked up for three Julys this time. Then he'd get out and open the juke joint again. Next, they enacted another town ordinance declaring alcohol illegal. Locked up for five Julys. On and on this went. Until Anita finally told Gerald to stop, they'd made enough money to buy a house to fix up and settle in, they could make their money another way. Through all those Julys gambling and alcohol was legal across the bridge. The casino was built in Gerald's second to last stint.

When Gerald was locked up, Sunday afternoons after lunch, Rocko would take Anita for a ride on her motorcycle. Anita never forgot the feeling of wrapping her tiny arms around that big woman's leather coat. Of the cool, clean air whipping her floral headscarf. Of the feeling when they were engulfed in the forests at the top of the Hills, the romance of trespass, the wonder of love. Everything felt new then. Of Rocko's flannel on her breasts when they lay on top of each other and kissed and watched the sky turn from pink to charcoal, each star opening itself, crystalline, bright. When the pink fog didn't cover the starshine. She called things off with Rocko for good the last time Gerald got out. To this day, it felt fated, even though it was a tremendous heartbreak. She lost track of Rocko, eventually, over the Julys. The feeling Anita holds on to, even today, is the complexity of love, and how she can easily hold love for many people at once. This kind of intimacy is not an obstruction, but a blessing, and she is blessed to have had so much of it in her lifetime.

The first time she and Gerald ever kissed was in this graveyard so many Julys ago, the night of Mildred's funeral. Mildred, Willie Earl's wife, was killed, somehow, by somebody, for who knows what, because she never wronged anybody, just as sweet as she wanted to be. Mildred and Anita grew up together, played hopscotch and basketball together, painted portraits together, and even sang together at the juke joint almost every night. Willie Earl had been in love with Mildred since she gave him a tiny pepper plant in the third grade. They took care of it together, even when they grew up and got married at the juke joint. At the wedding, Mildred and Anita sang a song they wrote for Willie Earl called "Us to Dust," about how Mildred and Willie Earl's love had grown like their peppers, and will keep growing until Willie Earl and Mildred turn to dust. Willie Earl cried so hard with his head in Gerald's chest, which made Gerald cry too, tears falling into Willie Earl's hair.

Anita wanted to go to Mildred's funeral, but her body wouldn't let her get off the couch until night. Gerald was on his way to bring some oxtails to Willie Earl, hoping they'd make him feel a little better. Gerald was cutting through the graveyard, and found Anita crouched over Mildred's grave burying coin in a fury, mumbling indecipherable words into the fresh funeral dirt, and that's all she felt like she could do was give something to Mildred she could take into the afterlife.

"Anita, what are you doing!" Gerald said.

"Noneya," Anita said.

"Anita! What are you doing!"

"Noneya!"

"Woman!"

"Listen here muthafucka," she said. "Don't call me Woman. You know my name. But don't say it again. I heard you the first *and* second time."

"Anita," he said. "I'm fretting about you. You know what people are saying."

"You tell THAT muthafucka I said to mind his damn business," she said. "That Is What I Am Saying."

"Anita, be reasonable," he said. "Get off the ground. Stop digging in the dirt."

"And you tell THAT muthafucka I said watch his mouth," Anita said.

"Anita! Please," he said.

"You tell THAT motherfucka I'm comin for his ass, he betta get out of town before he gets what's coming to him."

"Anita, what are you even talking about."

"No sir, not this time, no sir."

Gerald crouched close to Anita grabbing her elbow, her muscular arms and hands slung deep into the hole she'd dug. Gerald leaned into her, wiped a stray blotch of mud from her cheek, and kissed her lips only lightly, allowing the Holy Spirit and the wind and the trees and the grave dirt to rest between them.

"Anita, come on home now," Gerald said.

For the first time in Anita's life, she felt fully seen, fully cared for. As Gerald helped her up onto her feet, shook the grave dirt off her dress, took his cap off his head and wiped the back of his neck with his hand in relief, she knew Gerald was the person who could talk some sense into her when she ain't got no sense. The person who would support her, but keep his distance to let her fully be herself. She saw something different that day in Gerald, as he stood in the trees' shadows, lighting a cigarette and offering one to an angel-statue gravestone, and saying aloud to it, "Oh, you quit? Probably better, smoking kills you," and chuckling to himself. He was a good man, and he was the one.

In this present moment, Auntie Anita twirls into his arms and kisses him, fully and with intention, covering their heads with her shawl. She still knows after all these years how much coin she has buried in this graveyard.

July 4

Once upon a time across the bridge from the dilapidated casino, Auntie Anita is boiling water, adding flour, stirring and stirring until smooth. She's making wheat paste. She tells Uncle Gerald to get the paint rollers and brushes from the cabinet.

"What time you meeting Cristal today?" Auntie Anita asks.

"Somewhere around one or two," he says.

"I'll be back around noon to take the baby out to play," she says.

Auntie Anita pulls coffee cans of wheat paste from under the cabinet, slaps the bottoms of the cans into her palm, and places them in a dirty green canvas bag. She slings the strap over her shoulder and kisses Uncle Gerald and Cora Mae on their cheeks.

"Maybe I'll bump into y'all's weird-ass friend while I'm out there," she says to Otis and Joy, who are untangling fishing nets for her.

"Anyway, shouldn't it be *your* friend since you the one who been dreaming about her?" Joy says. Auntie Anita laughs and walks out, leaving the fishing nets.

Auntie Anita's newest art form is wheat pasting, and she was in the habit of pasting at night across the bridge, but the cops started watching too closely, sending more officers than usual on foot and bikes, which means anybody can do anything at night in Tannery Bay because all the cops are busy looking for whoever is papering up the town. Now Auntie Anita papers during the morning, the asscrack of the day she calls it, right after all the cops change shifts. She knows it's not dangerous because no one expects an old woman to be the one papering FUCK YOU AND JULY using her own hand-drawn letters framed by roses she stenciled herself on the police station and the tannery. When she makes art in her neighborhood, she only papers or paints or sculpts scenes of togetherness: dancing, hugging, sitting on porches, playing cards, eating around large tables. Or the giant rainbow trout nobody has ever seen. Or huge portraits of folks in need of peaceful memoriam, remembrances she calls them.

Willie Earl says the portraits of folks are judging you because you fucked up, or watching over you because you fucked up. Once a week Willie Earl walks the kids and the teens through the neighborhood, and always stands scratching his gray beard and pointing upward to the mural saying, "Check this out, youngbloods. Look into this person's eyes and feel deep within yourselves when you notice the subjectivity change, when you can't tell if you looking at the portrait or the portrait is looking at you." He laughs his giant laugh and walks away, but his laugh stays with the kids with its arms around their shoulders.

Willie Earl then walks up the street to the side of Harold & Hattie's Haberdashery and stands in front of the large mural of his wife, Mildred. He looks at her smooth, brown, peaceful face and soft eyes until she looks back at him, and Willie Earl feels like a mural—large and colorful and soft and highlighted in all the best places—and it's here in this plane, this plane of porousness between worlds where Willie Earl knows Mildred isn't dead. He cries gloopy paint tears until his laugh leaves the kids and returns to cradle him like a baby.

Today when Willie Earl melts inside of Mildred's mural, he feels something off. There's a damn disturbance, he thinks as he's floating inwards, toward the center of the mural, and he's looking around to find this damn disturbance and sees his overalls change into a dark-blue suit with gray pinstripes and a pink paisley tie. Nice threads, he thinks, still floating until he lands on the yellow patch of paint where he usually meets Mildred for a dance. She isn't there. But he sees a head pushing up through the yellow paint and he wants to stomp on it because it ain't Mildred's head, Mildred don't have wet stringy hair. It's the woman in waders standing in front of Willie Earl, motioning to his suit. He says, "I do look nice, thank you, young lady. Now where's Mildred?" She gives Willie Earl a cockle shell and lowers herself back into the yellow paint. Willie Earl's laugh reaches in and pulls Willie Earl back onto the street in front of the mural. He has on his regular old overalls again.

Other places across the bridge, Auntie Anita sculpts symmetrical symbols made up of triangles and circles connected by lines with some X's here and there. Auntie Anita says she doesn't know what they mean, but she feels like she needs to mold them because they are in her somewhere, like her song. She leaves little statues of symbols on gravestones, in the alley behind the casino, on manhole covers in the middle of the streets, on the concrete pillars beneath the bridge, at street intersections. She's calling to something through these symbols, even if she doesn't know what, or who.

Auntie Anita walks back in the house at noon like she never left, canvas bag empty. She tells Otis to bring more flour home from the dumpster in the casino alley when he goes back to work. She tells the same to Joy. She plops down in a chair and Cora Mae climbs into her lap. Uncle Gerald stands over the stove, tasting the broth from his oxtails, fixing everyone a steaming bowl before he leaves to meet Cristal. He hugs Otis and Joy like they are stuffed animals, then he kisses Cora Mae and Auntie Anita on their foreheads. After kissing Auntie Anita he wipes his lips with his forearm and says, "Sweaty-ass forehead, you musta been working hard."

Cristal sits by the bay's edge across from the casino and throws rocks into the most purple parts where it looks like oil in a rainbow surface skimming the top. When she was young, she and her friends would swear there was a monster in the bay, a dinosaur history left behind. The chemicals on the water hold the rocks a second longer than normal, like gel, plunging them to the bottom slowly. There is a rumor a coworker at the casino tried to have sex with the water once because he said it felt so good, held him so tightly, but the coworker adamantly denies the rumor, and Cristal feels he would tell her the truth of whether he tried to get down with the gel-water chemical bay or not. She laughs as she throws the next rock, watches it sink slow. Vaginas don't feel like gel-water chemical bay shit, she thinks, and it's clear he ain't never even been inside one. She wipes her hands on her jeans; her red nails are chipped, due for a new manicure. She knows she's going to rip the rest of the color off with her teeth anyway so there is no use in keeping up with it anyhow. The air only feels cool to her down by the water. The water alleviates the heat, even though to even be near it feels dangerous. The same coworker who ain't never been in a vagina swears the scars on his arms comes from being in the water, the chemicals eating his flesh. Cristal thinks, so I don't know. Bad fucking water.

She wraps her body around itself, pressing the bones of her chest into her knees, letting her light red, curlyhead rest, closing her eyes for a minute. She can hear the barge downriver, the chug

chug chug of the motor. She unclenches her jaw, relaxes her eyebrows, it feels good, she thinks, to let the body go. She thinks about Lexus, her round belly, her thin shoulders, and her long neon green hair that she never does anything with. She thinks about her crooked smile, her chipped front tooth, such a curved dent looking almost natural in her mouth. Her heart-shaped lips, a movie star. Her blue Dickies work pants, her blue Dickies work shirt with the name Gary in a red oval on the left side. Cristal wants to kiss Lexus every single time she sees her. Lexus has no idea how Cristal feels, and she will soon, she thinks, as she kicks the sand in a childish fit. Lexus is so cool, and just like generally never causes a ruckus except in love. She is always in love with somebody new! I love Lexus, though, like I really love her, and I want her to be with me, only me. She pulls out the small notepad she scribbles all her thoughts in and writes on her to-do list between Buy Milk for Auntie and Return Book to Joy as number eight: Get a Grip on Yourself, Girl.

The bay starts bubbling at Cristal's feet. When she looks at the horizon, there is the woman in waders walking on water. Cristal closes her eyes. She tries to breathe deeply, but her breaths keep catching in her throat. She opens her eyes and the woman is still there, coming faster toward her. When am I going to tell Lexus I love her, she thinks. She gets up and tries to breathe deeply again like Lexus taught her, letting the air fill her down her back and up her neck and holding it for two counts before slowly letting it out until the next breath is organic and a type of buoy. I gotta get to Uncle Gerald, she thinks. She runs away right as the woman in the waders reaches the shore, sprays her legs with bay water, and disappears.

Uncle Gerald is already sitting on the concrete seats in the first row of the old amphitheater with a small pot of oxtails, two bowls, and two spoons. Cristal walks in scratching at her legs, smiling a little. She sits and Uncle Gerald says, "You smiling because you and Lexus finally going together? You asked her? How'd you do it? Like how you practiced on stage yesterday?"

"No," she says. "We're not going together yet, and I didn't ask her."

"Ah, fine, fine, you'll do it when you ready," Uncle Gerald says, spooning some oxtails into Cristal's bowl. "Why you smiling?"

Cristal slurps some broth straight from the bowl and nods her head to let Uncle Gerald know the soup is good as usual. "I don't know, things are starting to feel funny. Over at the bay in front of the casino right before I walked over here this woman was walking on the water coming at me. She sprayed my legs." Cristal shows Uncle Gerald the red splotches on her ankles and shins. "Do you believe me? I swear it happened."

"Well goddamn! We been seeing her too!" Uncle Gerald flails his arms but accidentally knocks the pot of oxtails over. The pot clangs on the ground and the broth splashes like liquid usually does, but it starts to wobble and collect itself into the shape of a cockle shell.

"Let's get out of here," Cristal says.

Uncle Gerald rubs his shoe into the cockle shell-shaped broth. It splashes out of shape again but pulls itself back into the shape of a mason jar, changing to the distinct golden color of Uncle Gerald's hooch. His throat tightens and eyes widen.

"You said that right, Crystal!" Uncle Gerald says. He bends to pick up his pot, but shakes his head no. "You can stay here," he says to the pot. "I ain't bringing this bad juju back in the house."

They leave the amphitheater. Back on the bridge, silent even though they're never silent when walking home. Cristal says finally, "Who is the lady, anyhow?"

"Hell, I don't know," Uncle Gerald says, "maybe she's Saint Whatever-the-Fuck-You-Need to whoever sees her. I need a new pot to cook my oxtails in." He cups his hand around his mouth and yells over the bridge into the bay, "I need a new pot, Saint Lady!"

Cristal does the same, "I need a girlfriend, Saint Lady! And a whole buncha other stuff too!"

"I think the woman got something to do with Anita, some-how, some kinda way."

Cristal leans over the rail to spit into the purple bay, and notic-es four of Auntie Anita's small statues of people standing in a row at the base of one of the concrete pillars. The statues are in various poses—hands on hips, hand covering eyes shielding from the sun, arms spread for a hug to no one, fishing but leaned back like a big fish is on the nonexistent line. Cristal hears a deep bloop in the bay a little ways out and lifts her head to see, but nothing. When she looks back at the statues, they are huddled in a circle with their arms on one other's shoulders, and the tops of their heads touch-ing. She blinks hard and shakes her head, and the statues are back to standing in a row in their original poses.

"Uncle Gerald, wait!" Cristal jogs to catch up. "Speaking of Auntie, did you hear about the casino owner is taking credit for Auntie's art again? Now he's built a room sticking halfway into the alley. He's charging those rich folks up in the Hills an arm and a leg to see it, some kind of 'VIP exclusive' ticket scheme. I know you said you needed to figure out a way for Auntie to get some of the money."

"I saw that mess in the newspaper. You know they been doing it for forever, taking everything everybody else do, like they did with my juke joint."

"What are you gonna do?" Cristal says, stopping to pull Uncle Gerald's arm.

"What do you mean *me*, goddammit. This is a *we* situation."

"Well, what are *we* gonna do?"

"This what Imma do, Imma go to that casino, bust up in that muthafucka, steal all the coin from all them slots, then flip over all them blackjack tables, then go the office, steal the safe, strap that muthafucka to my back and crawl my big ass out—"

"But, Uncle Gerald—"

"Hold on, I'm on a roll . . . then Imma drag that safe across this goddamn bridge to the house and dump all the money in Anita's lap, cuz you know she gives and gives to everybody so we gonna give her something back."

"I don't know about all of this."

"And *then*, Cristal, you and your lil girlfriend are gonna blow up the casino, the newspaper office, *and* the goddamn tannery."

"It's getting kinda late tonight, Uncle Gerald, but okay, I'll blow whatever up tomorrow."

"No matter what, we should be the ones taking people to Anita's art, right? I mean, who else knows it better than we do? I don't know, let's talk to Joy and hatch a plan. We just gotta keep this from Anita cuz we gonna surprise her with a lot of money."

He rubs his hands together and puts his arm around Cristal's shoulders, and she puts her arm around his waist. They walk a little further down the bridge into the graveyard.

July 5

Once upon a time in a graveyard next to the dilapidated casino, Uncle Gerald and Cristal are cutting through, walking back to Bowfin Street from the amphitheater, when one of Auntie Anita's sculptures has come to life blocking their path. The sculpture is a young black woman and her beaming infant son: two neighbors shot by police. Auntie Anita formed them with teal robes, halos of stars around their heads, rods of gold behind them, lightning coming out of her son's hand, a crescent moon under her feet. The sculpture has ripped itself out of the ground where it has lived next to the haberdashery for who knows how many Julys, and here it is in the pink fog of the graveyard dancing, the child cooing in his mother's arms, the mother's robes glistening in the sun, round and round they go.

Gerald's eyes start to burn, and then itch, and then water. When Cristal looks up at him, he is crying. She grabs his hand. Cristal's eyes start to burn and itch, too, and tears she can't control start rolling down her own face. She feels the darkness in her belly roiling up through her sternum, into her eyes, as if this is the first time she has ever cried in her life. She feels the sun on her face. She thinks about Lexus. How much she loves her. She thinks about Uncle Gerald and Auntie Anita, Otis and Joy and baby Cora Mae, and how much she loves them. She feels overwhelmed with love. She can't believe her luck, how much she loves. It almost feels like love shoots out of her feet like galaxies, sending her to live in the Milky Way.

They stand in the middle of the graveyard, weeping together, transfixed by the holy ghosts. "Auntie Anita is never going to believe this," Cristal says.

Uncle Gerald winks at her. "Oh, she just might," he says, "she just might."

Once Uncle Gerald and Cristal are back on Bowfin Street, still weepy in front of their house, Charlene walks around the corner.

"What's wrong, baby girl?" Charlene asks.

Cristal stops crying immediately and says, "Everything is wrong, mom. I mean Charlene. Leave me alone." Charlene tries to hug her but Cristal pushes her arms out of the way and walks inside.

Charlene starts to follow, but Uncle Gerald steps in front of her.

"I know you trying, and I know it's hard, but she ain't ready yet," he says.

"I know, I know, thank you, I know, I know," she says. She walks away.

Uncle Gerald picks up the *Tannery Bay Daily* and walks upstairs. Cristal is sitting by the window watching Charlene leave their block. Cristal starts to say something but can't. She tears at her cuticles, makes herself bleed, shoves her pinkie into her mouth. Uncle Gerald sits the newspaper on the windowsill and hugs Cristal. "Quit pickin at your skin, girl. You alright," Uncle Gerald says. After he lets go, Cristal looks at the newspaper and says, "Oh my god."

Tannery Bay Daily

SPECIAL EDITION

WEATHER
Potential thunderstorms with golfball-size hail possible in Tannery Bay

ALL THINGS TANNERY BAY

TANNERY BAY, JULY 5

10 CENTS

New JULY Mural in Tannery Bay

Another JULY mural has surfaced overnight on the side of Tannery Bay Casino. The yet unidentified artist has become abstract over the course of the year with symbols of triangles, X's and circles. Although The Owners of Tannery Bay Casino claim the rights to the work because it is on their property, the question continues about who actually owns the rights to the art, which is generating rapid attention: Does the public? Does the artist? Do The Owners? Who will profit from the work? "VIP tickets remain available," The Owners told Tannery Bay Daily during a conference call this morning.

We are OPEN FOR BUSINESS

Cristal frisbees the newspaper across the room. "Can you believe it? We gotta figure something out fast."

Auntie Anita walks out of the bedroom carrying buckets of new wheat paste. "What is all this racket? What are you throwing around, Cristal? And what in God's name do y'all need to figure out?"

"Oh, nothing much," Uncle Gerald says. "We just tryna figure out a way for Cristal to talk to Lexus. She been practicing at the amphitheater, you know, practicing her love speech. She really got a good one. She ready."

Auntie Anita sets down the buckets, takes the brush from behind her ear and puts it in the front pocket of her painter's overalls. "That girl got your nose wide open, Cristal. Woo wee! I been there before, though. I remember Rocko had my nose wide open, too. You better start making sense of it, though, because you can't let love get away."

"You're right," Cristal says, glancing at Uncle Gerald, impressed with his save.

Later, Cristal comes out of her room, gives Auntie Anita money for rent, catching a glance of her mom walking by on the street below, dressed in her favorite low-cut blue jeans, black tennis shoes, and a cropped black T-shirt with T-BAY in purple cursive written across the chest. It's what Charlene wears when she is doing good, when she is feeling good, when she is the best receptionist at City Hall, when she has a place of her own instead of hopping between different friends' houses sleeping on their couches. She has retired, for the moment, the outfit she wears when she's down-and-out: dirty white flip-flops, oversized stained white sweatpants, and a faded fatigue jacket that is always buttoned to the top. Cristal never trusts the times she seems to be doing better because the dark times follow close behind.

As her mom leaves, Joy, Otis, and Cora Mae come into view. They cross the street from their building, coming over to Auntie Anita and Uncle Gerald's for dinner. Otis carries Cora Mae on his shoulders because everyone likes carrying her so much, and they're all laughing. Willie Earl is at the card table on his balcony, laughing the hardest, his head thrown back so his laughs bounce off the pink-smoke sky and disperse until they get lodged in the thick of the purple water. When bubbles pop you can hear the degraded decibel chorus of Willie Earl's laughs. They say Willie Earl's laugh fights the demons in the bay. They say his laugh is a flaming blue ball floating in his belly made of all his ancestors' sorrows and joys. When his wife died, Willie Earl didn't laugh for two straight Julys, and Bowfin Street was cold. The third July without her, in the middle of the night, his laugh came rumbling from way up in the Hills, swept over the bay like a hurricane, tiptoed through the graveyard, then slammed down in the middle of Bowfin Street so boisterous and booming it woke everybody up. From their front porch, Uncle

Gerald and Auntie Anita watched Willie Earl walk into the middle of the street and hug his laugh. Willie Earl and his laugh started dancing, twirling, dipping. Everyone else on Bowfin Street came outside to see the dancing. Then, everyone joined in, and they all danced till daybreak.

When Cora Mae was a baby and wouldn't stop crying no matter who sang or bounced or rocked her, they'd summon Willie Earl's laugh to rock and coo at her. Anita says part of Willie Earl's laugh stayed inside of Cora Mae. "That baby been here before, she done seen too much," Auntie Anita says, "and ain't none of us seen as much as Willie Earl's laugh."

Joy, Otis, and Cora Mae walk in the house and hug everyone. Auntie Anita opens the window and yells across the street, "Willie Earl, you eat yet?"

He says, "Not yet!"

"Get on up here, then, it's gettin cold!"

Willie Earl pulls some daffodils out of one of the pots on his balcony, walks across the street, takes them upstairs, gives everybody flowers and hugs everyone. They all sit around the table: Auntie Anita, Uncle Gerald, Otis, Joy, Cora Mae, Cristal, and Willie Earl. In the middle, steaming on a platter, is cornmeal-fried crappie Gerald caught in one of his secret spots yesterday, and he and Cristal cleaned, scaled, and fried them. Anita made cornbread, which sits next to the mason jar full of glowing hot sauce Willie Earl makes from the same pepper plant Mildred gave him long ago. The peppers are long and thin and curled at the end, glossy stripes of yellow-orange-red-green. Some people talk to their plants. Willie Earl laughs to his plants.

After Auntie Anita yelled for Willie Earl to come eat, she left the window open. From the street, Charlene's voice and cigarette smoke floats in, "Cristal, I'm trying, I'm trying. As soon as I get more money. I love you. Cristal, I love you."

Cristal folds a few crappies and squares of cornbread into a cloth napkin and takes them downstairs. Nobody looks out the window because it ain't none of their business, except for Cora Mae, because everything is her business. She yells out the window, "I love you Charlene—Happy Birthday, I'm glad you got borned."

When Cristal comes back up a few minutes later, Joy says, "Charlene's voice sounds like your grandma's. When she used to babysit me and Otis, she'd call us when it was time to be done swimming, and the same voice and cigarette smoke that came through the window just now used to come out into the water and wrap us like an arm and pull us to shore."

Willie Earl adds, "Her voice sho'll is alive." Everyone else nods in agreement. "Speaking of alive," Willie Earl says. "Anita, you know them sculptures of yours, the one of the woman and her baby, the ones who got shot by them cops? I saw 'em dancing around in the graveyard, justa twirlin."

Uncle Gerald and Cristal look at each other, and at the same time they say, "We saw it, too!"

Anita laughs with a mouth full of crappie, while drizzling hot sauce on a new piece on her plate. "Y'all just now seein, it's been happenin for a long time. I thought it was something only I could see."

Cora Mae gets down from the table and starts spinning around singing, "I can see it all the time, all the tiiiiime, alllllllll the time."

"Why didn't you tell me, baby?" Anita says lifting Cora Mae into her lap.

"I don't know why we can see it now," Willie Earl says, "and I don't care, I'm just happy to be in the presence of what you do. The woman and her baby was a turning point in the narrative you been building all over town, the visual coherency with the light had been somewhere in all your stuff you made around the same time, it's like the story is light, and light is the story!"

Everyone nods in agreement but Otis who drifts away in the dream of Willie Earl's words, and now he's sad the words have stopped, so he blurts out, "Keep going, Willie Earl!"

But Willie Earl doesn't hear him because he is also lost in the dream of his words, his mind back at his wife's mural and he keeps speaking from the porous plane. "Whatever you do Anita, and however you do it, shifts the subject of painting and viewer, we think we're looking at the people in the painting but they are really looking at us, so who is really being created, who is the object? Maybe we are."

Uncle Gerald, with his mouth wide open full of food, says "That's it, I got it!" and claps, snaps, and points two fingers at Willie Earl whose laugh is on his shoulder doing a two-step.

July 6

Once upon a time on Bowfin Street, across the bridge from the dilapidated casino, everybody wakes up all at once from the same dream.

First Uncle Gerald and Auntie Anita. Uncle Gerald jerks his sleep mask off and shakes Auntie Anita awake. Auntie Anita says nothing but reaches for him with her eyes still closed and there is his chest, his thick waist, his round cheeks. She cradles his face in her hand, and Uncle Gerald puts his hand over hers, closes his eyes. They listen. The chimes. The chimes are out front on the porch, and the couple is way upstairs in their bedroom, a lot of wood and carpet and doors and hallway between chime and ears. For one flashing moment, Auntie Anita is scared, but she squeezes Uncle Gerald's cheek and he pats her hand and holds it. There in the darkness he squeezes her hand three times, which is the way they say I love you with nobody knowing. Squeeze, I, squeeze, love, squeeze, you. She feels the sentiment settling across her sternum and into the blades of her shoulders and arms like a warm blanket. Nothing to fear. If the angels are coming, let's hope their wings are big enough for us all, she thinks.

Cristal woke up having kicked all of her blankets onto the floor, her head toward the foot of the bed and her feet near the headboard. Filled with anxiety, she moves outside to pick flowers in the small yard next to the house. The moonshine through the pink fog guides her way without a light. She laughs to herself as she adjusts her eyes to the dark, the streetlight blinking on and off. She likes her bedroom, Otis's old room. Uncle Gerald and Auntie

Anita allowed Cristal to decorate the room however she pleased. "It's your room," Uncle Gerald said. "Let it be yours." She painted the walls neon green. She loves music so above her bed went Sister Rosetta Tharpe, her mouth and her guitar midsong. On the wall across from the bed the concert poster from the Velvet Underground over her desk. On the back of her door, Jim Morrison with his shirt off which Auntie Anita once looked at and said "Boy could eat crackers in my bed any day, but don't tell Gerald," which Cristal thinks about at least once a week. On her nightstand is a small framed photo of her smiling grandma, Pearl Anne, with one arm around her smiling mom, Charlene, who's holding a smiling toddler Cristal, standing in the middle of bay bridge under a pale-pink sky. Another photo on top of the dresser drawer she took with her when she moved out of Charlene's apartment is young Uncle Gerald in suspenders and Auntie Anita in a polka-dot dress looking fresh and vibrant in front of the bar at the juke joint, with child Charlene with her blond curly hair, and child twins Otis and Joy, who, even though fraternal twins, looked a lot alike back then, shiny brown foreheads underneath big afros.

She finishes a bouquet she's going to leave on Lexus's doorstep. In the distance, the chimes sing sweetly, but there is no wind, and no way they could be tinkling in such a way.

Across the street, Otis jerks his head up from his chin. He fell asleep reading, his book in his hand, sitting straight up with his glasses still on his face. He didn't intend to fall asleep, but sleep overtook him like a lover, seducing him until his chest concaved and his body went limp. He wasn't even really reading, but thinking about his future—boo thang, Leviticus. He imagined him, as he often does these days, Leviticus living in his perpetual memory. He imagined him getting ready for bed in the bathroom—the noises his toothbrush might make, the gurgling and maybe he'd be singing while he washed his face, singing while he moisturized. The way he would turn the lights off with feather fingertips. The same fingertips with the small scars from needle points he saw projected on his blackjack table. The way he would carefully untuck, unroll the sheets, stack the decorative pillows neatly on the chair, slide in and over to Otis in one fluid motion, tuck his body under Otis's arm, his belly pushed up against Otis's legs, his thick legs curled up by his side like a spiral, all without saying a word as to not disturb his reading. He imagined how he smelled, like cologne and Florida Water, and all the time, no matter when he saw him. Flowers and gorgeous.

Otis would put his book down, take his glasses off, and they would make love. Ew, he thinks to himself, *make love* is so gross. He shakes his head. Before his nightly imaginings, he didn't remember the moment he fell asleep, or what paragraph he was on. No matter, he dog-ears the page, sets the book down on the nightstand, folds his arms above his head and closes his eyes. He searches his mind for what woke him, for if he could return to the moment in his imagination when he gets on top of Leviticus. This is something he wants to return to, something that feels so good, but also fills him momentarily with dread, or is it excitement? Uncle Gerald is always telling him to look at his fear as excitement, not everything has to be scary all the time, and maybe his nerves are telling him to be elated, to be eager, to be happy. These two emotions, Uncle Gerald said, can be confused in the nervous system.

Otis feels the confusion deeply in this moment. The fear and excitement making him gasp. He takes off his glasses, folds them on his chest, puts both hands on top of them. If there is a god, Otis thinks, which I don't think there is, but if there is one, and you can hear people, and he laughs and rubs his nose, and I don't think you listen to us a lick, but if you are listening, and on the off chance that you are a real thing, please help us get out of July because I'm so tired, so goddamn tired. Bring Leviticus to me. He swears he can hear Auntie Anita's chimes in the wind, trickling in from across the street. He puts his glasses on top of his book on the bedside table, turns off the lamp with three small clicks.

Down the hall in the primary bedroom, Joy wakes up but immediately tries to go back to sleep. Next to her Cora Mae lifts Joy's eye open. "Mama, are you in there?"

Joy says, "Yes baby, I'm in here, come on," and grabs Cora Mae and pulls her into her chest, hearing the chimes bounce and echo in the vaulted ceiling.

When Cora Mae's daddy Juice, Joy, and Otis bought the place, they agreed that Otis preferred the smaller room. Joy loves the private bathroom, big windows, and the farmhouse sliding door Otis and Juice pulled from an old barn and mounted themselves under the supervision of Cora Mae, who was saying, "Too high, Uncle Otis, too low, Dad, that's not right, paint it orange, no paint it rainbow." And they stained it rainbow.

"Mama," Cora Mae says. "The lady was in my sleep."

"What lady?"

"The lady scares you, Mama—my friend."

Joy feels her eyes involuntarily widen, wraps her in the coforter. "Oh yeah, what did you do?"

"I said happy birthday, I'm glad you were borned," Cora Mae says.

Joy kisses her forehead. "What did the lady do?"

"She smiled and gave me a big, fat, giant hug. How she know me, Mama?"

Joy can feel Cora Mae's hot breath on her cheeks. She don't know you, Joy thinks, she don't know any of us. Cora Mae rolls out of Joy's arms and Joy feels the emptiness, the emptiness of Cora Mae's daddy joke-complaining about Cora Mae rolling all over the bed. "My little pinball," Juice used to say, his hot breath on Joy's cheeks. It's been ten Julys and Joy continues to let her mind drift back to the night at the tannery, their overnight shift.

Joy presses both hands to her chest, trying to add some heaviness to the emptiness of Juice, thinking about him folding her into his chest the same way she does to Cora Mae. She starts crying because she can't grasp the full weight and image of Juice. She grabs Cora Mae again for some real weight and hot breath. "I love you, my little pinball."

Here is the same dream waking everyone else, except each person says something different to the lady in waders, and her response is the same: she smiles and gives each of them a big, fat, giant hug. In his dream, Uncle Gerald said, "Whassup, Saint Lady, you got my new pot with you?" and she smiles and gives him a big, fat, giant hug. In her dream, Auntie Anita said, "I've been dreaming of you since I was kid," and she smiles and gives her a big, fat, giant hug. In her dream, Cristal said, "I miss my mom," and gives her a big, fat, giant hug. In his dream, Otis said, "Show me how it gets better," and she smiles and gives him a big, fat, giant hug. In her dream, Joy said, "Show me how it gets better," and she smiles and gives her a big, fat, giant hug.

"You was only dreamin," Joy says to Cora Mae, "and dreams ain't real."

"No, this was real, mama."

Joy knows it's real too, and it scares her, but she says, "Shut your eyes now, baby, let's rest. Let's play the quiet game, see how long we can stay quiet."

After a while, Cora Mae's little arms are relaxed over Joy's stomach, she is snoring lightly.

In the pink morning, Auntie Anita rolls over and goes back to sleep. Uncle Gerald walks out the bedroom to find Cristal waving at Otis in his window. Otis waves back thinking, I hope that girl quits askin about what to do about goddamn Lexus again, she got one more time. She already took my room, and now she takin up all my nerves.

Joy walks over to the window and waves at Cristal, thinking about how Charlene went downhill after her mom—Cristal's grandma—died. Joy and Otis didn't think it was a good idea for Auntie Anita and Uncle Gerald to let Cristal stay with them because Charlene might cause too much trouble for everybody, but Uncle Gerald told them, "Now, I know you know how much her grandma watched y'all when y'all couldn't even piss straight, so we are going to do the same."

Joy keeps thinking back to how defensive Auntie Anita and Uncle Gerald get about Cristal's grandma, Good Ol Pearl Anne, and the stories about her and Auntie Anita running hooch from Uncle Gerald's juke joint to spots all over town.

Auntie Anita always tells one story about how the cops caught on to them crossing the bay with cases of hooch and would search their boat. Luckily, the first search happened on one of their midnight "dummy trips"; Auntie Anita always did air quotes when she said "dummy trips." The "dummy trip" was a trip across the bay to the fishery. Auntie Anita said the cops stopped her and Good Ol Pearl Anne in the middle of the bay, boarded their little boat and searched everywhere, and she'll say the next part with a laugh, "and all they found was clams and cod!" The cops took all the seafood that they had paid good money for. But after that, Good Ol Pearl Anne had an idea about how to get the hooch across the bay even if the cops decided to stop them again, which they did. She bolted two steel loops to the bottom-middle of the boat, and sealed them with tar to make them watertight, then covered the tarred bolts with a painted wood panel to make a false bottom. She threaded thick ropes through the loops and tied the cases of hooch to the rope with weights in the bottom of the cases so they wouldn't float. They hung a fathom below the boat. This is when Anita would clap her hands, "We dragged them cases smooth across that muthafuckin bay and them crooked-ass cops ain't know a goddamn thang!" Auntie Anita and Good Ol Pearl Anne would make a couple of trips per night, stashing the hooch in the hidden floor door of the fishery. At dawn, when it was time for Good Ol Pearl Anne to make her deliveries for the *Tannery Bay Daily*, she would pick up the stashed night hooch and deliver it with the papers. Anita would slap Gerald on the shoulder: "We had all these muthafuckas around here reading a lil news and having a lil nip at the same time! Gerald made it, but if it wasn't for us, he wouldna sold shit." Then Gerald would always say, "You sho'nuff right about that!"

Gerald taps Cristal on the shoulder. "Did you hear how Willie Earl was talking about Anita's art last night?"

Cristal says, "Everyone knows he loves her art. Why do you ask?"

"Shhh," Gerald says. "I don't want Anita to hear. Let's go over to Otis and Joy's, and I'll tell you more."

Once they cross the street, Willie Earl is sitting at the table on the sidewalk in front of his balcony, peppers blooming behind him. He says, "Good morning. Thanks again for the fish last night, Gerald. Tell Anita I'll be looking for more of her art. Or her art will be looking for us, HAHAHAHAHAH WHOOO HAHA-HAHA!"

Willie Earl's laugh follows Gerald and Cristal up the three flights of stairs and blows open Joy and Otis's door. Cora Mae is on the living room floor playing with wooden blocks and humming Anita's song. Gerald bends to kiss her, then tells Otis and Joy to get out the window and come sit on the sofas with him and Cristal. He tells them about what he and Cristal talked about while crossing the bridge after the bad juju happened at the amphitheater. He says him and Cristal got something cooking, they want to get Anita some money somehow, "We gotta be the ones taking people around to see Anita's art, kinda like how Willie Earl is already doing with the kids."

Joy says, "How about a bus tour? Since I know the folks from the Hills ain't gonna wanna be walking around like the kids do."

Otis follows along skeptically.

"Whether it's a walking tour or a bus tour," Uncle Gerald says, "the key to this plan is Willie Earl. Did you hear how he was talking about Anita's art last night?"

"So what?" Otis says. "He always talks about Auntie's art."

Uncle Gerald runs his hand over his forehead and eyes, "He does, but not in that sorta fancy way he did last night."

Otis leans forward, inspecting Uncle Gerald's eyes, "You started making hooch again, Uncle. Are you drunk? Ain't nobody got time for this foolishness."

"Looka here snot-nosed chumps," Uncle Gerald says. "This *can* work. Check it out: nobody knows Willie Earl, so being anonymous is our best weapon. Nobody knows Anita is the one making all this beautiful shit. So we gonna train Willie Earl how to be a lil more sophisticated so he can pose as the artist's agent. He can already talk the talk. We just gotta put some fancy threads on him and teach him how to walk the walk. We gonna turn him into some big shot art agent who's mad because people are profiting from his client's work."

They all look at each other, considering it. Otis says, "Naw, it ain't gonna work, have you even asked Willie Earl?"

Uncle Gerald doesn't say anything, but immediately stands, walks to the balcony, sticks his head over and yells, "Willie Earl, come up here, lemme rap to you for a few ticks!"

July 6 [reprise]

Once upon a time on another July 6, up the street from the dilapidated casino at the tannery, Joy stood in front of her workstation with her hands on her hips and leaning forward. She told Juice, "I don't give a damn what the Owner said, it ain't safe to go down there and work on them pipes at night."

"He threatened to fire me, he said it was urgent," Juice said, shoving a wrench into the back of his tool belt, then dusting it off. Joy rolled her eyes at him trying to keep the damn tool belt dust-free at a time like this.

"He's never here, how does he know what's urgent?"

Juice said, sighing, "He's probably never even been down to the pipes to know what the conditions are like, but I gotta go. I'll be safe."

Juice was being safe. He was always safe. He went down to the pipes, attached the safety harness to his tool belt, and clipped to the welded railing as usual. He climbed down into the pipe system. He saw nothing wrong. Nothing clogged, no foreign-object debris, no foreign-object damage, everything was good, nothing was urgent. He tapped his wrench on the walls of the pipes and the tinny echo boinged until it got tired. He put the wrench back into his tool belt and dusted it off.

Back up top, next to the valve releasing chemical liquid from vats into pipes, was a red light. Everyone who works at the tannery knows the lit red light indicates there is someone inside the pipes. DO NOT RELEASE VALVE. But the Owner, who never showed his face there, who wanted to prove his power, who sent Juice into the pipes in the first place, did not know what the red light meant. Joy saw him across the room reaching up to the lever. She yelled a sharp "Stop!" but he didn't hear her and pulled the lever down, shooting a vat full of purple chemicals into the pipes. Joy ran over, tackled the Owner, hopped up, and turned the valve off. It was too late. Joy and the other workers ran into the pipes. Joy found Juice drowned, his harness still attached. She cradled his head to her chest and stroked the side of his face. The purple liquid subsided around them, flowing out into the bay.

In a press release in the *Tannery Bay Daily*, the Owner denied all wrongdoing, calling Juice's death a "senseless tragedy" caused by "insubordination." He sent Juice's family "thoughts and prayers." When the community was outraged and seeking justice, confronting the Owners about putting the responsibility of Juice's death on Juice and not himself, the factory, or the ignored safety precautions, the Owner doubled down. He sent a basket of fruit to Juice's parents after the funeral, every piece bruised and rotted. Joy never forgave the Owner, the tannery, every person complicit in the death of her boyfriend, her daughter's daddy. He was a good man, and did not deserve to die in such disrespect.

Next to his workstation, which was adjacent to her own, their coworkers made a makeshift memorial, until the Owner's son complained and the Owner demanded it be dismantled for "safety reasons." Before it was dismantled, Joy would light a candle and talk to Juice's picture—a photo of him smiling big, playing with Cora Mae. She would ask for strength, for justice, and for the ability to keep her wits about her as she faces every day at that goddamn tannery without him.

Joy talks to Juice daily, all of these Julys later, in the few minutes she has after she leaves Otis to clock in at the tannery and the few minutes she has alone after she clocks out before she meets Otis to walk home. Juice always told Joy that Cora Mae was destined for great things in this life, so long as we could get her out of July.

July 7

Once upon a time in the junkyard at the end of Bowfin Street, Gerald, Cristal, Otis, and Joy stand in front of one of the old city buses, one not as broke down as the others, but still rusted in spots with busted windows and a missing hood showing an engine that might be worth a damn, its tires stuck in the red clay underneath it.

"What y'all think?" Uncle Gerald says.

"It's doable," Joy says, looking at the other buses. "We can pull parts from wherever and make it work."

Cristal steps inside and sits in the driver's seat, grabs the steering wheel, and says, "And I can definitely drive it."

Otis shakes his head and rolls his eyes. "Alright, let's get to it, Joy."

Yesterday morning, after Uncle Gerald rapped to Willie Earl for a few ticks, Willie Earl said, "I'd do anything for Anita, I'd give her my pinky toe if she needed it." Joy and Willie Earl sat at the kitchen table collaborating on a letter for the newspaper.

They spent the rest of the evening having Rashaad's Towing tow the bus out of the mud to drier land, while Willie Earl and Uncle Gerald scoped out the rest of the busses in the junkyard for the parts they needed, a carburetor here, a knob there. Willie Earl and Rashaad Thompson, the owner of the junkyard and the tow truck, go way back, so he handed over the keys to Willie Earl saying, "If you can make that ol hunk of junk work again, by all means, and take anything from anywhere on the property to make it work. I owe you." Willie Earl laughed his ethereal laugh which floated

out into every corner of the junkyard and stayed there all day long. Willie Earl could not for the life of him remember why Rashaad owed him and for what, but he thought, who am I to argue with Rashaad, and took the keys anyway. When we get a good chunk of change, Willie Earl thought, Imma bring a pillow sack full of cash to Rashaad for his kindness.

The next day, they got to work. The bus would sputter and die, sputter and die, so Willie Earl, Uncle Gerald, and Joy spent the day figuring out what needed to be replaced and how and why, scouring the rest of the junkyard for the parts needed to make the thing. Cristal and Otis spent the day inside the bus vacuuming and pulling seats out and putting seats in, cutting and sanding wood trim, fixing the sunroof, replacing windowpanes, and calibrating the latch for the emergency handle on the back door.

It was hard work, but fun work, everyone breaking out into Anita's new songs and Anita's old songs from the juke joint, Uncle

Gerald's reverb underneath the hood singing, "Shake that shuga to left, shake that shuga to the right." Joy dancing with her cleaning rag in her hand, whipping it around in the air, harmonizing with him. Willie Earl's laugh flying from the far reaches of the junkyard into the bus and back again. Uncle Gerald saying, "I know we all having fun, but remember, this is our secret. This is sho'll nuff gonna be a good surprise. My baby gonna be happy!"

At the end of the day, Cristal decided to stay the night in the bus, to camp out under the stars. It felt safe enough, no one talked her out of it, and Rashaad approved. She borrowed a sleeping bag and pillow from him, made a little bed on one of the bigger seats, and closed her eyes.

She couldn't wait to see Lexus tomorrow at the casino to tell her about the bus tour, and how it was about to unfold. She trusted Lexus with her life. Cristal heard the cicadas one by one begin to beckon each other. She smelled the trees, new blossoms above the faint rotten-egg smell of the tannery. She saw the stars bat their eyes slowly. She could taste the acid from the bay, a hot purple bubble rising in the back of her throat. The hair on her arms raised a bit, goosebumps from neck-to-knee. She sat up, looked into the darkness of the bus. Her eyes adjusted on the woman in waders. Standing in front of the woman was a hologram of Charlene and Lexus, pulling a pie made of gemstones out of her Good Ol Pearl Anne's oven.

"Why do you keep coming around here? What do you want from us!" Cristal yelled, out of character and thoughtless. Charlene and Lexus dropped the pie, and sliced pieces rose suspended, sending kaleidoscopic rainbow shadows all around the bus, bright enough Cristal had to shield her eyes. The bus floated. Cristal closed her eyes.

July 8

Once upon a time in the morning in Rashaad's junkyard, Cristal wakes up to Willie Earl's laugh shaking her shoulders and jumping up and down on the bus, even though he is standing outside. She stands up. The bus is sparkling vinyl and shined chrome, no indication of a life before the junkyard or inside the junkyard.

"Maaaan, this ol thing looks like it just came off the lot, woo wee son we did it!" Uncle Gerald claps Willie Earl's back.

Willie Earl is bent over, his head between his knees, "I can't believe it and wouldn't if I wasn't seeing it with my own two eyes, how in the world, what on earth," he says.

Cristal puts her jeans on, adjusts her shirt so she's decent, and runs down the walkway rubbing her hands on the soft blue interior fabrics, marveling at the shininess. She opens the bus doors, clamors down the steps, jumps the last one.

"Cristal!" Uncle Gerald says. "Come over and look at this." The three of them stand in front of the shiny new bus, sleek and beautiful. "Well, let's start this mothafucka!" He takes all three of the steps up inside in one leap, sits in the big leather driver's seat, sticks the key in the ignition and turns. It purrs and hums. "Smooth as a baby's punkin head," he says, and gives Willie Earl and Cristal a thumbs-up. Willie Earl's laugh dances a two-step behind him on the seats.

Otis and Lexus are getting off work at the casino, standing on the sidewalk waiting for Joy to reach them. Joy walks up and hugs Otis, says hi to Lexus while scrunching her eyebrows. "This is weird, you're not usually here," Joy says.

Lexus says, "Tell me about it—I saw the woman last night. She showed up at foot of my bed, and casted out of her hands a hologram of Cristal holding my beating heart in her hands. I went to go throw my pillow at her, and I realized my pillow-case was full of cockle shells. I didn't know everyone else has been seeing her too! Otis said I had to come and tell you all today." She pulls a cockle shell out of her blue Dickies shirt's front pocket.

Otis holds up a cockle shell, "And the woman left this on my blackjack table."

Joy sighs and pulls a cockle shell from the inside pocket of her leather coat, "Same."

On the way back to Bowfin Street, Otis, Joy, and Lexus cut through the graveyard, and beneath the pink sky, a purple fog settles so thick they can only see the arched tops of the gravestones. Sitting on one is the woman in the waders flashing a scene in her eyes of a little girl walking on water.

"Oh hell no!" Joy says.

The woman says nothing, but her eyes keep replaying the same scene.

"You ain't gonna keep coming around not sayin nothin," Joy says. "Ol rude ass."

Otis grabs Joy's arm, "You probably shouldn't be cussing out a ghost."

"Shut up," Joy says. "You scared of every damn thing." She cups her hand around her mouth and yells, "Ain't nobody scared of you but Otis!"

Lexus says, "I think he's right, Joy."

Joy snatches her arm away from Otis and starts walking through the fog toward the woman. The woman disappears.

Joy yells, "That's what I thought!" She throws the cockle shell toward the gravestone where the woman was sitting and it vanishes into the fog with a purple puff.

"Let's go," Joy says.

Lexus punts her cockle shell with her foot toward the purple puff still lingering, making Joy laugh and say, "Aww yeah, Lexus, get her!"

Right when Otis opens his mouth to say "Damnnn y'all!" he reaches into his pocket to feel three cockle shells. He runs ahead of them instead of saying anything. He doesn't want to be anywhere near any of it.

"Where you going with your old scaredy ass? Otis! Come back!" Joy yells after him.

At Uncle Gerald and Auntie Anita's house, Cora Mae walks into Auntie Anita's room and whispers her hot breath in Auntie Anita's face, "Auntie, Auntie, I gotta go peeeee."

"Go on ahead, baby," Auntie Anita says.

"I want you to come with me, I gotta go peeeee," Cora Mae says.

"Gerald, get up and take this baby to pee, please," Auntie Anita says, feeling an empty bed over on Uncle Gerald's side. "Gerald?"

"He ain't here," Cora Mae says.

Auntie Anita takes Cora Mae to the bathroom where she finds a cockle shell on the back of the toilet. As Cora Mae pees and sings her songs about her friend, the lady in the waders by the bay, Auntie Anita pauses for only a moment when she swears the baby's song turns back to one of her own songs as if she was never singing about the woman in the waders by the bay. Auntie Anita lets her sit on the toilet for a minute longer while she splashes her own face and neck with water in the sink. When she's done, she gets Cora Mae off the pot, washes her hands, dries them, and hoists Cora Mae onto her hip.

In the living room, she opens the curtains facing the street. Below to the left, coming from the junkyard, she sees Cristal smiling while walking behind Willie Earl and Gerald, who are dancing together in sync: right step forward, hip shake clap, left foot forward, hip shake clap, lean back. Auntie Anita can't hear what they're saying which is: "Ain't nobody in the world, fuckin with Earl and Gerald."

"And Cristal!" Cristal says.

"And Cristal!" they repeat.

Auntie Anita looks at Cora Mae and says, "What them fools up to, baby?"

"Bus!" says Cora Mae.

Anita looks back out the window and sees Joy, Otis, and Lexus walking from the right. It looks like Joy and Otis are arguing. Lexus is shaking her head like she's had about enough.

"Now look at these other fools," Anita says to Cora Mae.

"Fools!" says Cora Mae.

Anita watches them all meet in the middle in front of Otis, Joy, and Willie Earl's apartment building. Cristal, eyes bulged, is gesturing wide with her arms to Joy and Otis which makes Gerald and Willie Earl start dancing again. Lexus is fixated on Cristal but still looks confused. Joy and Otis look annoyed. Otis picks up a newspaper off the sidewalk and says, "Let's get out of the street, people gonna think we more deranged than they already do."

Upstairs in Joy and Otis's apartment, everyone sits around the coffee table filling Lexus in.

Joy takes the paper from Otis and starts to read:

The Owners Respond

Joy says, "You can hear the punk-ass in they voice, they scared scared. Otis did you help them write this? They fell for it, now all we gotta do is wait a few days to reply, let they lil fear keep building and building. In the meantime, Willie Earl, I mean Mr. Townsend, I gotta teach you some sophistication and shit, baby!"

Willie Earl's laugh responds for him, jigging across the hardwood, sliding into the wall.

Lexus looks at the ceiling behind her green bangs, then says, "There seems to be a problem. What if Anita reads the papers and sees all this back-and-forth about her art? She'll know it's about her for sure."

Cristal puts her hand on Lexus's knee and says, "Lexus, Auntie doesn't bother with the papers. She even kicks them out of the way whenever they're in front of the house."

Otis, Joy, Willie Earl, and Uncle Gerald exchange glances while passing the paper back and forth, hoping what Cristal said stays true.

July 9

Once upon a time in the graveyard next to the dilapidated casino, Cristal watches Lexus sidewalk surfing with her boys. One by one, they balance off of a large Mother Mary statue, and when it comes to Lexus's turn, she misses the landing, and falls onto her back while her skateboard rolls forward. The rest of the boys laugh, and one offers his hand to her, dusts off her back, but runs to catch up with the group. Even though it is hot outside, Lexus wears a jean jacket with all kinds of different patches, and Cristal thinks it's so sexy, even though Lexus is sweating her ass off, her hair half-shaved and sticking to her neck. Lexus starts to talk, and a piece of hair falls into her mouth, but she keeps talking.

"I made this for you," she says, and pulls out a cockle shell-and-macramé necklace. "I found a bag full of shells on the street in front of the school the other day, right in front of the statue of all those men playing horns." Overnight, a statue went up in front of the school made of dark gray metal and clay, men of different shapes and sizes attached at the knees playing saxophone, trumpet, trombone, and tuba. Cristal swore she could hear the music in her mind, as if the neon psychedelic notes floated out and over to occupy the spaces in her brain.

"Will you put it on me?" Cristal asks. Lexus drops her board hard to the ground, moving closer. Cristal can smell her Old Spice aftershave, a welcome smell to counteract the tannery-stink air.

Lexus moves to the back of her. "Can you lift your hair up?" she asks and proceeds to gently lay the necklace over her throat, securing the cockle shell clasp. "It's a little loose," she says, and frowns.

"I still really like it," Cristal says. "Thanks for thinking of me."

Cristal shivers from the pink breeze coming through the graveyard. Lexus's friends are well ahead of them, not paying attention to if they are following or not. Usually, they all will continue down the path, through the iron gates at the south end, to the street adjacent to the junkyard where they will cut through the gardens and to the other side of the block where they will scatter to their houses and sit down to dinner with their families, watch television, go to bed, just like every July 9th. Except, this July 9th feels different.

"Are you cold?" Lexus asks. She takes off her jacket which lifts the T-shirt underneath up a little, and Cristal can see the mole on her rib cage, and her pale bra. She pulls her shirt down while she hands the jacket to Cristal.

"No, you really don't have to, I'm fine," Cristal says.

"I insist," Lexus says. "Please."

Cristal puts the jacket on. It's baggy, comfy, smells like Lexus. Cristal knows, from this moment on, she never wants to be without this smell. Lexus smiles, and Cristal's heart melts.

"Can I kiss you?" Lexus asks.

Cristal nods, and they kiss next to the mausoleum. Lexus's lips are slightly dry, and her mouth tastes like butterscotch candies and cigarette smoke. Cristal already has to reach up on her tiptoes to kiss her, but she reaches further to kiss her again and more on her cheeks and neck and eyes and forehead. They both laugh at the shower of kisses. Cristal loses her balance, falling forward. Lexus grabs her elbows to ensure she doesn't fall on her face.

Right then, a rustling sound from the trees behind them starts, and squeaky crunching like boots on glass. It is getting dark outside, and they can't see beyond the end of the mausoleum too well.

"Who's there?" Lexus yells, dropping Cristal's hand and picking up her skateboard. A hollowed-out shape appears in the pink fog, as if something invisible is standing there.

"Show yourself, dickface," Cristal yells.

From the mist, a woman's head appears, dark stringy hair and tan waders. Before they can see the rest of her, Lexus picks Cristal up in her arms, gets on the skateboard, and starts to glide toward the graveyard gates, pushing her leg as fast and hard as she can. Cristal watches over her shoulder the top of the woman's head become smaller and smaller. They hold hands as they walk the few blocks home, but don't say a word about the woman.

Later on, getting ready for bed, Cristal undresses in front of the mirror and puts her hand to her throat. Her necklace is gone. She checks all of the pockets of Lexus's jacket, shakes the rest of her clothes out, looks up and down the stairs and around the front door so carefully Gerald asks, "What are you looking for, child?"

"Nothing," Cristal says.

"Well it ain't nothin, ain't nobody looks for nothin that hard," Gerald says.

Anita laughs and hits Gerald and says, "If Cristal didn't have a neck to attach it to, she'd lose her head, I tell you what." They laugh together as if they both heard the funniest thing ever, as they always do, and Cristal rolls her eyes. They are the funniest people they know right now, she says to herself as she goes back to her room.

As she closes the door, a reflection in her mirror catches her eye. When she gets closer to the bed, she finds a single cockle shell on her pillow, so delicately placed in the middle it hardly causes a dent.

July 10

Once upon a time across the bridge from the dilapidated casino, across the street from the graveyard, and next to Merle's Plumbing, Joy and Willie Earl stand on the sidewalk looking at the window to a brick storefront. Peeling gold leaf letters on the window read: Harold & Hattie's Haberdashery. Merle sticks her head out her door and says, "Go on in, they're in there." When Willie Earl and Joy walk inside the faded forest green door, the bell at the top dings, and dings again upon closing. They stand by the door touching dusty black and blue fabric for suits folded on tables and hanging from wooden shelves on the wall. They rub the silk ties and handkerchiefs between their fingers in the wooden trays. The chest-and-torso-only canvas mannequin stuck full of pins sits on a platform near the back by a staircase.

"Hello," Joy says. "Anybody here . . . Hattieeeehhh!"

No one answers, so she walks over to the stairs and yells up, "Hellooo . . . We wanna buy somethin!"

A woman's voice yells back, "Give us one second!" followed by a man's voice "Who ain't lock the door?"

Willie Earl walks to the fabric hanging from the walls, running his hand along a dark blue material with gray pinstripes, "This is nice, this is real 'phisticated, whatchu think Joy?"

Joy comes over to inspect, holds the fabric against Willie Earl's bearded cheek. "The blue goes nicely with your skin, and the pinstripes complement the gray in your beard."

Willie Earl walks over to the table with the ties, and picks up a diagonal-striped light-and-dark blue tie.

"Nah," Joy says. "Too businesslike, you need something a little more eccentric that speaks to the art agent part of you," she says hovering her index finger over the choices. "This one right here!" The tie is pink with blue paisley.

Hattie finally comes down the stairs, did up nicely, her graying blond hair in loose pin curls, pearl earrings, and a double pearl necklace over a fitted forest green sleeveless dress. "Good morning, Joy and Willie Earl," she says. "We haven't had customers in who knows how long. What can we do for you? Well, there's this one woman who comes—" Hattie stops talking and turns to look when she hears Harold coming down the steps. "Oh, it's only Harold," she says. "You never know who's coming down those stairs lately."

Harold's little white afro is picked out and shiny, and his blue suit matches Hattie's heels, his silk green tie and pocket square match Hattie's dress, his pearl cuff links on his crisp white shirt match Hattie's necklace. "Look here, it's Joy and Willie Earl," he says. "I didn't know it was y'all, I would've cleaned up a little quicker! What y'all need?"

Joy holds up the fabric. "We need a suit for Willie Earl."

Hattie lifts her eyebrows. "What do you need a suit for, Willie Earl?"

"Umm, umm . . . ," he says, "for some art stuff."

Joy sighs, then runs the plan down to Hattie and Harold. "But please, whatever you do, don't tell Auntie, we don't want her to know."

Harold says, "Know what?"

Hattie says, "You have our word—and speaking of your Auntie, she was out back painting on our building this morning. We haven't seen it yet, but I'm sure it's beautiful as always. We should all go see it after we're done."

Harold and Hattie take Willie Earl over to the platform with the mannequin by the stairs. They put on glasses and pull out measuring tape, both walking around Willie Earl studying, making him lift his arms, spread his legs, lift his chin. Joy remains standing by the ties watching them work on Willie Earl when she hears the ding of the door opening. She turns and sees Harold and Hattie's son, Leviticus, who is taller than both his parents, carrying a stack of flattened cardboard boxes with rolls of brown tape on the top the same color as his curly afro. He has on a blue tank top and gray sweatpants. Harold yells out, "Thank you baby, but no packing up today, Willie Earl needs a suit!"

Leviticus and Joy hug, and Joy says, "I haven't seen you in a while, how you been!"

"Good, good," Leviticus says. "Dealing cards as usual. I'm on a different shift from Otis, so I don't get to see him but only in passing. How's he doin anyway?"

Joy smiles. "Otis is good, as a matter of fact, he told me to tell you hi if I saw you here today, so 'Hi' from Otis."

Leviticus smiles shyly. "Really?"

"Yeah boy," Joy says smacking her lips. "He's always asking in behind you, talking bout he needs to request a shift change again so he can be on your shift."

"Dang!" Leviticus says. "We must've requested shift changes at the same time, because I requested a shift change so I could be on his shift, and when my shift got changed he was on my old shift."

Joy says, "You know, we're having dinner tomorrow, you should come through."

Leviticus perks up even more. "For sure, you think Otis will be okay?"

"Ha! Okay? It was his idea! He told me to tell you hi and to invite you over for family dinner."

Willie Earl yells, "My hot sauce will be there, too!"

Hattie and Harold finish measuring. Harold says, "Come pick up the suit tomorrow evening, what else we got to do? You gonna be the sharpest beak on the block, Willie Earl!"

Hattie says, "Now let's go out back and look at Anita's mural." Hattie, Harold, and Leviticus walk out first, with Joy and Willie Earl behind.

Willie Earl whispers to Joy, "Otis finally built up the nerve to invite him over, huh?"

Joy whispers back, "Hell no, I lied my ass off, you know he too scared."

They're all outside, standing in a row, looking up with their mouths open and eyes wide: a mural of Willie Earl in a dark blue suit with gray pinstripes and a pink-and-blue paisley tie with a matching pocket square. He's framed by intertwined vines of his chili peppers.

Once they get back to Bowfin Street, in front of Anita and Gerald's house, Willie Earl whistling the Chiffons's "One Fine Day," the temperature drops so it no longer feels like July. The air crisp, red hard leaves tinkling on the ground behind them, following closely. The sound is so assured, it sounds of footfalls, as if someone is following them. Joy looks back every now and again, but it's nothing but leaves.

"Alright, Willie Earl," Joy says and squares off with him in the street, stepping in front of him, making him lose his tune. "We have to work on you being an art agent."

Willie Earl puts his hands on her shoulders. "What do you know about being an art agent?" His laugh is on top of the roof, his laugh is slam dunking a basketball in the middle of the street, his laugh is riding the back of one of the red, hard leaves settled in the gutter near them.

"More than you!" Joy says. She lifts his left hand from her shoulder and kisses it tenderly. "Do you know what you need to do?"

He pats her right shoulder and puts his hands on his hips. He lifts his hand, shields his eyes from the sun, looks up into the gathering dark clouds in the west. "I can't say I do, but I do know how to talk about Anita's art. Boy, her art speaks to my soul."

Joy sits down on their building's front lawn, waves at a neighbor passing by walking her dog. Willie Earl tips his hat in her direction and sits next to Joy, digs into the dirt with his shoe.

"All you gotta do is make the Owners convinced Anita's art is worth a lot of money, that Anita is the artist to watch out for in Tannery Bay, that those rich folks up in the Hills want her art, that they would be missing out on the greatest up-and-coming thing to happen to the art world if they don't act now. But, you gotta speak their language. You can't be cussing, and don't drop your *g*'s at the end of words. Matter of fact, over-enunciate your *g*'s, *and* your *r*'s, white people love that shit. Don't be saying shit like 'grinnin' like a oppossum eatin a sweet tater' or 'finer than a frog hair split four ways.' Don't be calling them folks no gooseneck peckerwoods and slew-footed heffas and trout-mouth heathens—don't call them nothing but sir or ma'am. If you see a woman with a big ass walk by, you better not fix your lips to say 'she sho'nuff draggin that wagon.' Keep your sassy ass focused, Willie Earl!" Willie Earl's laugh bounces from house to house, windows to windows, rattles foundations, so thunderous.

"Come on, you tryna change who I am, Joy. I cain't just change who I am."

"No," Joy says, "I'm trying to get us a bunch of money. You already know how to talk about Anita's art. Now, you gotta sell it. And you gotta sell it to the Owners in a way that makes sense to them: You gotta talk exclusivity. Rarity. Money. Profit."

"Alright, alright." Willie Earl smooths his hair with both of his hands, one right after the other. Takes his chin in his fingers and cracks his neck to the right and then to the left, scratches behind his ear. There are no bugs in this July, no mosquitoes, no bees, and he loves it, he thinks, there are other Julys where he just got eat up, but not this July. He threads his fingers behind his head and lays down in the grass.

"Tell me what I gotta say, and I'll say it. Let's get this money, Joy. I'm ready. I'll do whatever you tell me," he says. "I can't wait to wear that suit, though! I'm gonna be looking finer than a frog's hair, cooler than the other side of the pillow."

Joy rolls her eyes, hits him in his ribs. "Can you not?" Joy says.

"Oh, right," Willie Earl says.

"Let's go in," Joy says, "so Otis can give you a haircut, plus I gotta tell him about his upcoming date anyway."

Joy and Willie Earl walk up to find Gerald, Otis, and Cristal sitting at the dining room table with a spread map of the Tannery Bay Hills.

Gerald looks up, "We figuring out bus routes and times."

Cristal runs her index finger along the main road winding through the Hills. "I'll start here and stop at the end of the street at every switchback."

Otis rubs his chin. "I like that, but I think you should stop in front of every house, door-to-door service to make them feel special."

Cristal nods, "Good point."

Joy asks Otis to cut Willie Earl's hair.

As Otis ties a towel around Willie Earl's neck, Joy says, "Otis, I bumped into your future boo at the haberdashery. He asked about you."

"Leviticus?" Otis says, lighting up.

"I told him you told me to invite him over for dinner."

"Oh shit!" Otis says letting the clippers slack and drop in his hands. "Now he's gonna think I really did."

"That's the point, Otis! You're welcome."

"Don't you go messin up my 'do with your love business," Willie Earl says, his laugh on the map walking the main road winding up through the Hills.

Otis buzzes on the clippers and starts trimming the back and sides of Willie Earl's gray hair, fades it into the top. He stops the clippers and pulls out his straight razor to give Willie Earl an edge up.

Joy says, "Now you can hear, Willie Earl, listen up. You gotta go into this meeting and control the space, the flow of conversation. Remember, you'll already have an advantage, so don't mess around. First is names—they gonna try to call you Mr. Townsend like they did in the letter, but fuck that, I want you to say, 'You may refer to me as William Earl Townsend III,' make them hoes say your whole goddamn name."

Uncle Gerald yells from the table, "That's what I'm talkin about, Joy!"

Otis keeps scraping with the straight razor.

Uncle Gerald stands from the table. "Good good, we'll start the bus tour in the next few days."

Joy says, "Me and Willie Earl will work up an ad for the paper announcing the tour, and once the tour has been running, we'll respond to the Owners about meeting."

Meanwhile, up in the Hills, the Owners are having a meeting-before-the-meeting. A man in a lime green velour bathrobe skims a pool net on the top of his swimming pool, collecting leaves and beer cans. His eyes and mouth are caked with white crust. His nose is red and bulbous, and he picks it and eats it.

Meanwhile, another man with a huge bald spot in his white wavy hair and a pointy white goatee creeps slowly up the driveway in his car. Once up to the sprawling house he parks and walks the entire property line to get to the backyard between two persimmon trees where a rotten fruit drips onto his shoulder and down his back. He doesn't even notice.

Meanwhile, another man sets down his reflecting mirror used for tanning and, instead of getting up to greet Bald Spot 'n' Goatee, lays a towel over his eyes and farts.

Meanwhile, another man steps out onto the veranda from the house with a platinum tray adorned with golden chalices and large bottles of wine which he sets on the table and gently unloads, admiring each chalice and bottle.

Delores the housekeeper steps in front of Golden Chalice and begins to take away the tray, and he snatches it from her, forcing her to fall backward, another housekeeper catching her to break her fall. He sneers at them both, motions for them to leave.

Meanwhile, another man with a large birthmark on his neck loudly greets Bald Spot 'n' Goatee. He is cleaning a gun on a table far away from everyone. Occasionally he puts the barrel in his mouth when he thinks no one is watching. Golden Chalice begins to fill the cups and says, "Are all the Owners present?"

Meanwhile, another man floats on an oversize flamingo pool float and is looking at an XXX magazine as if it is a newspaper, licking his finger while he turns every page.

Meanwhile, another man dressed in black shiny shoes with greasy gray hair sits quietly at the table on the other side of the veranda. When Delores comes over to clear the glasses from his table, he pinches her ass. Delores catches his hand and bends his fingers backward until they almost break. She throws his hand down and continues to wipe the table. As she walks away, he scowls and nurses his hand, dipping it into the icy remnants of his gin.

Lime-Green Velour Robe says, "If we don't stop Townsend, there will be more Townsends!"

The other Owners all agree in unison, except XXX.

Lime-Green Velour Robe yells "Do you agree?" to XXX. XXX is startled and drops his magazine into the pool.

"Agree with what?" XXX says, reaching for the drowned magazine but not able to catch it as it drifts away.

Lime-Green Velour Robe's crust around his mouth starts to crack and ooze. "Do you agree Townsend and his client are preparing to sue us?"

XXX says "Wholeheartedly, absolutely, unequivocally, yes," as he sits back, exhausted from trying to catch his magazine.

Lime-Green Velour Robe wipes the pus from his lips. "Okay, what we are dealing with here are some high-powered and high-class people. We are more powerful. We own everything in this town. We are not going to let some flimflam art curator come in and control anything."

XXX says, "We can't afford to lose more smackaroos!"

Lime-Green Velour Robe says, "We will take all of his money and leave him homeless in the streets of Tannery Bay with nothing! He is finished! Through! A loser! We are the winners!" He picks up a two-pronged BBQ skewer next to the grill.

XXX says, "We must stop him!"

Lime-Green Velour Robe says, "When find him and the ding-a-ling artist, we'll string them right up!" He walks over to the fence, robe flapping in the breeze, and yells, "Do you hear me, Townsend? You rat bastard! I'm coming for you!"

XXX says "Perhaps we can countersue?" Birthmark with the Gun has moved closer to the rest of the men and rubs the same spot on the gun with his cleaning cloth repeatedly, sitting at the edge of a camping beach chair across from XXX.

Lime-Green Velour Robe walks to the other side of Birthmark with the Gun and slashes the flamingo float with the two-pronged BBQ skewer, the float losing air fast. XXX starts to panic.

"I can't swim!" XXX says, thrashing around as the float begins to sink beneath him. Birthmark with the Gun twirls the gun in his fingers and loses his grip on it before it almost falls. All the men laugh nervously.

XXX flails to the side of the pool, pulls himself up, sits on the edge dripping wet. "Countersuing does not seem a viable option in this particular situation. You'd only be countersuing for vandalism, which would only buy you removal and cleaning supplies. The costs to move the motion forward would exceed the amount you'd be awarded if you won the case for vandalism, which is highly unlikely," he says, humiliated.

Lime-Green Velour Robe interrupts him. "That's not good enough! These jerkoffs can't take what's mine!"

XXX says, "You mean ours?"

"Right, of course, ours. What are our other options?" Lime-Green Velour Robe flicks the pus away from his eyes.

Delores wipes down the table for the tenth time, all while being shooed by the other men to go away.

Shiny Shoes purses his lips, shuffles some papers, locks up his briefcase. "Our best option at the moment is to wait until we have a meeting with Townsend, and let him think he has complete control of the situation while we figure out how to defend our assets."

The flamingo float sinks completely to the bottom of the pool, gurgling all the way down.

July 11

Once upon a time on Bowfin Street across the bridge from the dilapidated casino, Auntie Anita comes home from sculpting and arranging more abstract symbols on a building. She goes to kick the newspaper out the way as usual, but an advertisement with a large photo of a bus with TOWNSEND TOURISTIQUES written on the side catches her eye. The advertisement says:

Auntie Anita folds the paper, carries it between her teeth because her arms are full, and walks up the stairs. Once there, she finds Uncle Gerald and Cristal sitting at the table talking and drinking coffee. They freeze when they see Auntie Anita. She spits the paper on the table with the front landing up.

"Gerald, the hell is this?" Auntie Anita says.

He picks up the paper, dramatically shaking it out, and lowering his readers to see the print better. "Oh wow, a new art tour, might be a good thing for the town. Would you be interested in going, Anita? I know you love art."

Auntie Anita sets down her buckets in the kitchen, stands in the doorway with her head tilted to the right like she don't believe a word coming outta his lying-ass mouth.

"Ohhh yeah, I heard about this new tour the other day, seems cool," Cristal says, trying not to make eye contact with Auntie Anita.

Auntie Anita looks at Cristal the same way she is looking at Uncle Gerald. "Y'all must think I'm Boo-Boo the Fool. I been seeing y'all sneaking around, whispering in the street. Who the hell is William Earl Townsend? Don't tell me you got Willie Earl up in this lil plan of yours. I'm the only one doing anything around this town," she says.

Uncle Gerald puts his hand on his forehead, lowers the paper to the table, takes off his readers and rubs the back of his neck. "Aw hell, Anita! Okay, okay, you got us. You wasn't supposed to find out, when did you even start looking at these newspapers?" he asks.

"To-damn-day, Gerald, that's when," Auntie Anita says. "Now, what y'all got cookin?" She moves a dining table chair around so she is sitting on it backward, starts drumming the top of it with her thumbs. "Cristal, I know ya lil ass involved, too, you and this old fool can't even take a shit without each other." She laughs and slaps her knees. Uncle Gerald laughs, too, but Cristal does not.

Uncle Gerald and Cristal run down the scheme to Auntie Anita, how it started, everything that's happened, everything they want to happen and think will happen, why they're doing it, and everyone involved.

Auntie Anita says, "Nope. I don't like this. We shut down the juke joint so we can live in peace, and now you wanna stir up again. I don't want it. Y'all better shut this down now. Go on ahead."

Uncle Gerald crosses his arms and shakes his head. "But Anita, them folks done already took everything from us, and here they are again, making money off your hard work, *your* art that *you* make for *our* community, *for us.*"

Auntie Anita says, "Next time you get hemmed up, who knows how many Julys you'll be gone for, and I ain't riskin it. I don't wanna lose our home, lose you, lose everything we've built for some dumbass tomfoolery over art I can take down in two seconds if need be."

Cristal raises her hand to speak, but Anita puts it down on the table for her.

Uncle Gerald laughs, "Aw, come on Anita, let the girl talk."

Auntie Anita says, "I do not, want to hear, another fucking word, from you, from her, from nobody. I'm done."

Cristal raises her hand again, and Anita slaps it down. "No," she says.

Uncle Gerald raises his hand, and Auntie Anita glares at him. Uncle Gerald says, "I feel you, but, you gotta understand. These owners are making money off your art, and you're not seeing a dime. Not a nickel. Not a goddamn penny. More importantly, all the people you love won't be able to see your art because the owners are controlling it all across the bridge, and you know it'll only be a matter of time before they bring they ass over here to control all of it."

Auntie Anita leaves the dining table, but not before she squeezes Cristal's shoulder lightly. She goes into the kitchen. She brings coffee cans and glass jars over to the sink, and starts mixing paint, the same paint she used for her mural of Mildred. As the paint swirls together, and drips from the sides of the jars, her mind goes to watching Willie Earl take the kids around the neighborhood to look at the art, and then she starts thinking about Mildred. I miss her so much, and so does Willie Earl, it's why he always ends the walk with those kids at her portrait, she thinks. She starts singing the song she and Mildred sang at the juke joint together. As she is singing, Willie Earl's laugh comes through the window from the street below and hits the high notes with her, before taking a seat at the table with Cristal and Gerald.

She washes her hands, wipes them on her canvas apron, and goes back to the table. She places her hands on the table and leans forward. "I kinda do miss scheming with you, Gerald. I'm in. I got some firm boundaries, though. Y'all better pay everybody involved, and pay'em good, don't be skimping on my account. Secondly, I make shit when and where I want, like I been doing my whole life, and ain't no silly-ass men gonna stop me. Y'all best figure around what I got to do. Yes? Let me hear y'all with your voices agree with me."

Uncle Gerald and Cristal say "Yes" in unison. Uncle Gerald gets up and hugs Auntie Anita tightly, so tight she laughs and starts pushing him away saying, "Goddamn, Gerald, get off me now."

"It all sounds right to me, baby!" Uncle Gerald says.

Delores and the girls and their shiny red bikes are leaned back up against the gas station wall, the sun lowering itself into the bay making them squint. Behind them, a wheat paste mural of two black children's faces, laughing at each other with mouths wide open, gleaming eyes, bouncing cheeks.

Delores cracks her knuckles, smooths the collar of her paisley shirt down, tucks in a part in the back that had scrunched up. She feels good because she's off work and don't have to deal with them folks up in the Hills. She feels loose tonight, boy, and she says it to her girls, "Babes, I feel loose tonight, like the world is opening for me," and she cracks open a can of TB Brew and gulps until it's gone.

Lexus, who's been hanging out more and more at the gas station because she wants to be part of Delores's crew, hands Delores another can covered in a brown paper bag, and she takes a drink, and it doesn't hurt until it does, at the bottom of her throat, coats her stomach, she hasn't had anything to eat all day. She doesn't mind, with the world opening up like this and all. Look at little Lexus, Delores thinks, trying so hard, but she's in and she doesn't even know it yet. Delores leans up against the wall, snaps her fingers, whistles at nothing.

Lexus and the girls are talking about the new bus tour in the Hills, thinking out loud, but not really listening to each other, about if they could get a gig with Townsend Touristiques. "Don't it just sound fancy as hell," Lexus says. Her voice is so big, it startles Delores sometimes, coming out of that tiny woman dressed in men's work clothes. She's looking great these days, Delores thinks, as she looks at her girls who are in various stages of drinking, smoking, talking, laughing. All of us girls are with our fades so high and tight, and our boots shiny, and our collars popped and locked.

Delores drinks again, says, "Y'all really wanna work for some bougie-ass art shit? What do you all know about art?"

"I don't know, I like that one guy who cut his ear off, what's his name? He cool," Rosalinda says. They all laugh.

"Yeah, he cool," Delores says, and gently hits Rosalinda on the arm. "He definitely cool," she says again. Delores is not an artist, not really a creative person, more analytical, numbers, she knows exactly how many pounds of beans and rice will feed people. "Art is not practical," Delores says, taking another swig, which stops the other girls in their conversation. She wasn't listening to them, and they weren't talking to her, anyway.

"What are you even saying, D? Ain't about art, this is about making that good money, trust and believe," Rosalinda says. "Anyway, about the bus tour . . ." and she turns her back to Delores. Which, at another time, would have made Delores jump out of her skin, how dare she disrespect her, but today, no, today, is a day of peace and prosperity, getting what's theirs, they are the Queers on Gears, Delores and the girls, they peddle their bikes around town, because it's safer and more environmentally friendly than motorcycles.

The pink sky is dissolving into darkness and the humidity makes eyelids stick every time you blink. Delores and Lexus hop on their bicycles and tell the rest of the homies they'll catch them tomorrow. They pedal along the cracked sidewalk contouring the purple bay. Delores heading back to her apartment on Bowfin Street to play spades with Willie Earl like she usually does. Lexus heading to visit Cristal like she usually does.

Delores slows down and says to Lexus, "You know, babe, I'm on to do bougie art if the rest of y'all are gonna do it, ain't nuthin wrong with making a few extra ducats."

Lexus nods her head in agreement, still peddling, thinking of course Delores would do it, she'd do anything to be able to feed a few more people. Lexus watches Delores look out past her to the bay, lost in her own thoughts of art and money, watches her peddling become more intentional, faster, when the air around them shifts. A cold zone. They can see each other's breath puffing white. The purple bay bubbles, slowly and then furiously, and with each pop of distant fireworks they hear Willie Earl's laugh rising into a chorus of echoes slightly soothing Lexus's fear, but not Delores because she's not afraid, she's locked loose into this moment, the world is opening for me, the world is opening, it's finally opening she thinks. With the back of her hand she taps Lexus on the arm over and over saying, "See, I fucking told you, the world is opening."

The bay bubbles, Willie Earl's laughter gets louder, and the woman with the tan waders emerges from the water with balled fists, stands in front of them on top of the water. Lexus can't move, her mouth open, even more afraid than the first time she saw the woman. Delores is rubbing her hands together, grinning. The woman levitates on top of the water, opens her fists, palms up, offering them each a cockle shell. Delores sets her bike down and runs to grab one. Lexus stays put, so Delores grabs the other one too, and shoves it into Lexus's hand. They turn their backs to the woman and examine the cockle shells, looking over at the other one's hands to check out each other's shells. Delores holds hers up to the sky to see what she can see. They hear the bubbling die down, and when they look over their shoulders, the woman is gone. They put the shells in their socks. Delores picks up her bike, and they start walking along the sidewalk. "See, babe," Delores says. "I told you the world is wide open." They are silent for the rest of the walk.

Charlene saw it all because she was sitting on a bench a little ways down, taking in the purple swirls of the bay as she does at this time of day. The woman in the waders appears out on the horizon in front of Charlene, and before Charlene can react, she projects onto the water a scene of Cristal's fat baby fists grabbing her index fingers and chewing on them to relieve the pain of her teething gums, which shifts to Pearl Anne's strong arms lifting toddler Cristal onto the kitchen counter to let her help bake a pie. The woman in the waders delivers these memories back to her today, and Charlene feels so grateful. When she can't remember anything good, she knows her life is and has been filled with beauty. The scene in Pearl Anne's kitchen switches to Pearl Anne with Cristal, both of them laughing and squealing in delight, Cristal's baby voice saying higher! higher!, and then Christmas, Pearl Anne and Charlene cheersing glasses of eggnog, watching Cristal open her presents, and finally the last Halloween of Pearl Anne's life when she made Cristal a rainbow trout costume. Cristal's cutie red cheeks. Pearl Anne's beautiful smile. How they all loved each other so much. Before the bad times came. Before she lost control. Before Cristal stopped wanting her around. These moments playing out in front of her so vividly, as if Pearl Anne was still alive. She wishes she could call her on the telephone, say Mama, I love you so much, thank you for everything. Instead she says it to the woman in the waders, Mama, I love you and thank you for everything. In the distance big rainbow trout jump, their scaly bodies gleaming with spectrum, but nobody sees them.

Charlene gets off the bench and starts walking toward Lexus and Delores, who don't see her, but they turn their heads in unison when they hear footsteps. Lexus is relieved it's Charlene and not the woman. Delores is disappointed. Charlene says, "I saw her too, and I saw her give you all something. I don't know what it is and I don't wanna know if you don't wanna tell me, and even if you did wanna tell me I'm still not sure if I wanna know, so just don't tell me."

Lexus feels around in her sock for the shell. "Nobody gave me nothing."

Delores pulls her shell out and says, "Oh, it happened alright, and I'm glad you saw, too, Charlene, and ain't none of us gonna sit here and act like it ain't just happen—she gave us these shells. I don't know what for, but a babe don't come up out the bay and give you a shell for no good reason, I know for a fact, jack."

Charlene touches the shell in Delores's palm. "Joy's little girl wears one around her neck, and Willie Earl has one in his pepper pot. I think it's the same woman Cristal has described seeing. We had a good talk the other day, Cristal and I, and she said Joy, Otis, Anita, Gerald, and Willie Earl have all seen the same woman. I thought she was a little bananas but now we're all bananas right along with them." Charlene looks down at her hand, a cockle shell in her fist she never noticed was there before. She had been clutching her fist so tight, the shell made an imprint on the inside of her palm. The water in the bay bubbles slightly like water brimming to boil on a hot stove which makes Charlene nervous. "My mama always said there was something strange in the bay. She knew."

"Strange for real, I don't think nobody seen these shells in a long time, or ever, they only heard about 'em. I saw one in an old fisherman's book. As much as I'm on Willie Earl's porch, I've never seen the shell," Delores says.

"I think it's because you can't see the shells unless the woman wants you to," Lexus says.

Delores bows to the bay. "She wants me to see it! I *knew* the world was opening for me."

Together they all start walking back to Bowfin Street, but they wanna hurry because they have so many questions they want to ask Willie Earl. Delores tells Charlene to sit on her handlebars, and they take off peddling until they get to the graveyard, foggy, cold, and darker than everything else like it has its own ecosystem. "Let's take the street around the perimeter," Lexus says, "I've seen enough to last me a lifetime."

Once they pull up to Willie Earl's ground-floor balcony, Lexus swings one leg over her seat and puts the kickstand down with the same leg. Charlene hops off Delores's handlebars, and Delores puts her kickstand down, shaking her head and already waving her arms around wildly. "Willie Earl, we got some shit to tell you!"

Willie Earl is sitting at his table with Cristal and Uncle Gerald shuffling cards. He stops shuffling and says, "Let me hear it!" Charlene shoots finger guns at Cristal, and they each nod awkwardly.

Delores hops the railing by gripping it with two hands and swinging her feet over, sits at the table. Lexus and Charlene lean over the railing with their elbows. Delores puts her hand on Willie Earl's shoulder. "We're riding home and this ghost babe busted up out of the bubblin-ass bay, just popped up in front of me and Lexus like here take these shells."

Cristal, Uncle Gerald, and Willie Earl crack up laughing. "Looks like she's been visiting all of us. I asked Rashaad and the old fisherman had they seen the ghost lady, and they hadn't," Willie Earl says.

Charlene claps her hands once. "See, I told you, Delores!"

Willie Earl leans over to take his cockle shell out of his peppers' soil, holds it up and says, "Don't nobody know what she even want, but maybe it means y'all are in it now."

Delores says, "In what, Willie Earl?"

Cristal relays the plan, the sightings of the woman, and how everyone involved has a shell. "Well hell," Delores says. Willie Earl's laugh takes the cards and starts shuffling, each shuffle a rumble of low giggle. "I was gonna try to work for the bus tour anyway, so can I get a job Mr. William Earl Townsend?"

"It ain't up to me," he says, placing the cockle shell in the middle of the table. "You gotta ask Joy, she got all the plans."

Delores puts her cockle shell in the middle of the table next to Willie Earl's. "Hold up, Willie Earl, how you gonna use your full government name for a scheme?"

"Ain't my full name," he says.

"What is your full name? Sir Duke of Williamson Earlis or some shit?" Everybody cracks up.

"Naw, it's just Willie Earl," he says, "just plain ol Willie Earl. Joy came up with the other name because she said it sounded high-saditty. Now, deal them cards, girl, or go on home."

Delores starts dealing the cards and says, "One more thing." She stops mid-deal as everyone slides their cards into their hands and gets busy rearranging. "If you gonna be the agent for this anonymous artist, somebody is gonna have to see this person with their own two eyes or they ain't never gonna believe you all the way. You need a decoy. I'll do it! Cuz I can be an artistic lookin babe if I want to. Y'all forget I work for them Owners! I'm at their house almost every day. I can keep my ear to the streets if you know what I mean. Y'all need me, son."

Willie Earl puts his cards down and moves his toothpick from one side of his mouth to the other. Cristal and Uncle Gerald shake their heads in approval, and Uncle Gerald motions Willie Earl to play the first card. "You do got a point there, D. A good-ass idea, a mighty good-ass idea indeed! HAHAHAH-WHOOO. Let's tell Joy!"

"Not yet," Delores says. "I came over here to bust some heads in spades first, now which one of these babes on your team, Willie Earl?"

Cristal raises her hand. "I am, and I'm good too, don't let the smooth taste fool you."

Delores says, "Girl, you been hangin around Gerald too long!"

July 12

Once upon a time on Bowfin Street, Anita and Gerald pull some extra metal folding chairs out of their closet. Lexus came over early to help Cristal set plates and cups and forks in the center of the table. Cristal thinks about standing on the bay bridge with Lexus, kissing her at twilight because people say twilight is a connection between two worlds, and if they kissed on the bay bridge during twilight that would be so symbolic—their worlds finally coming together as one.

Gerald's oxtails and onions and garlic and bay leaves and thyme are stewing. The fragrance billows fog out of the window and hugs the bushes and light poles and asphalt before spilling across the bridge through the casino and up into the hills.

Across the street, Otis hops out of the shower, wraps a towel around his waist, and starts dancing, unfolding the straight razor and retrimming his mustache in the mirror. Joy is sitting on the couch in the living room writing on index cards while Cora Mae yells over the balcony telling Willie Earl about a dream that she had, about a lot of people at the bottom of the water stuck in the mud.

Two floors up, Delores finishes getting ready, scrubs her boots to a shine, finishes ironing her Dickies pants.

Up the street across from the graveyard at the Haberdashery, Leviticus hops out the shower, wraps a towel around his waist, starts dancing, and picks his afro in the mirror. He gets dressed, goes downstairs and hugs Harold and Hattie. They give him the hat, the suit, and its accompanying accoutrements for Willie Earl.

Charlene is sitting on her favorite bench at the bay again, try-ing to figure out the best thing to say to Cristal that won't yuck her out. Don't come on too strong, show you're in a really good place, you really care, things are different this time around, she repeats to herself Auntie Anita's advice. An apparition of Pearl Anne appears, pushing a light-red-haired, pigtailed Cristal on a swing, and this memory projects itself onto the purple water, the toxic color makes the memory glow. Charlene feels ready, I can do this, I can do this, and gets up and walks to Bowfin Street.

Leviticus leaves the haberdashery, headed to Bowfin Street.

Delores and Willie Earl meet in front of their building, lock arms, and cross the street together.

Joy, Cora Mae, and Otis follow Delores and Willie Earl, and they all go inside Gerald and Anita's house.

Cristal sees Charlene walking toward the house and she runs downstairs and out to meet her.

"Hey Mama," Cristal says motioning to hug her but stopping herself. She instead shuffles her feet, doesn't know what to do with her hands so she puts them under her armpits. "How are you?"

"Nervous," Charlene says. "I'm not, you know, doing bad. I'm doing fine. Give me a chance, Cristal." Cristal cringes. The wrong thing to say, Charlene thinks, but she couldn't say anything else. She feels her body wanting to lean in for a hug but also stops her-self because she thinks it might be too much too soon. Cristal breaks and they hug an awkward hug.

Charlene and Cristal walk in the house. Otis hears the door open, gets up from the table, and walks to the top of the stairs to look down. He rolls his eyes when he sees it's Charlene and Cris-tal. Joy snickers silently, exchanging glances with Uncle Gerald. He tries to ignore her so he won't bust up laughing. Delores kicks Joy's feet under the table to get her to stop snickering. Otis walks over to the window to look out but he doesn't see anyone, then he sits again and starts tapping on the table.

"You okay, Otis?" asks Auntie Anita. "Don't worry, he'll be here."

He says, "I'm worried about this foolish plan, is all."

Willie Earl slaps Otis on the back. "It'll be fine, all of it, and that boy will be probably be here before I fini—"

The door opens and Otis gets up and motions for everyone to stay seated as he goes to the back of the stairs and sees Leviticus walking in.

"There you are, Otis!" Leviticus says, refusing to hide his eagerness.

"Heyyyy Leviticus," Otis says through the jittery vibrations of his vocal chords. "How was your walk, I mean, welcome to my house, I mean, to my Auntie's house."

Leviticus takes the stairs two by two and hangs the suit and hat on the coatrack. Otis reaches to shake his hand while Leviticus is spreading his arms for a hug, then Otis spreads his arms and Leviticus reaches out his hand. They chuckle and finally get in sync and hug each other, one of those good good hugs like trying to pull somebody inside of you. Cora Mae runs over, hugs Otis's leg, looks up at him, and says, "Ooooh he is pretty."

Leviticus squats and hugs Cora Mae, "Thank you, and you are pretty too! Is Otis pretty?"

Cora Mae says, "Nooo!" and runs to Auntie Anita.

"She's wrong, you know," Leviticus says to Otis. If Otis wasn't dark skinned you could see the blood blooming in his cheeks.

"Naw, she's right about you," Otis says.

Leviticus smiles and says, "You're too kind."

He removes the suit off the coatrack and presents it to Willie Earl, curtseying. "Your attire, King Townsend of Tannery Bay."

Everyone starts hollering at him to go try it on and show them. While Willie Earl is in the bathroom changing, Lexus and Joy go over the index cards detailing what she's supposed to say on the tour tomorrow while Cristal is driving. Cristal and Lexus are reviewing the route and figuring out what times they'll alternate driving. Cora Mae is sitting on Leviticus's lap while Otis steals glances, trying not to be too obvious. He can't help but look at Leviticus, and the way he is with the baby makes him that much more attractive. Gerald is filling up bowls with oxtails.

William Earl Townsend III busts open the bathroom door and comes out with the suit on struttin something awful, he got a glide in his stride and a dip in his hip. "Check out the pinstripes, baby!" he says, smoothing out his coat sleeves.

"Alright Willie Earl," Anita says. "I see you, lookin casket sharp!"

Delores tells him to spin around so she can see what her art agent looks like from all angles. William Earl Townsend III spins slowly with his arms out at his sides, then sticks one foot out so they can get a better look at his slick brown shoes. He screws it into the ground like he's putting out a cigarette, and starts sliding across the floor. His laugh unscrews the glowing hot sauce in the mason jar in the middle of the table.

Delores had spent last night figuring out what artists look like, rifling through old books. She has her artist outfit folded in a duffle bag underneath the table. When Willie Earl is done modeling, she tells everyone she'll be right back.

She goes into the bathroom and comes out with wrinkly black pants, a black trench coat, and black thick soled boots on.

Rosalinda's sister let her borrow a wig, white and curly, because of her recognizable fade, and big, black circular sunglasses that cover half of her face. To complete the look, she runs her fingers along the floppy brim of her black felt hat.

"I got the artist look down, right?" she asks.

"You sure do!" Joy says. Everyone else agrees and cheers.

"By the by," Delores says, "the toilet is stopped up, and I swear I only peed."

Anita says, "We know, damn toilet been giving us trouble for a while."

Gerald says, "Better call ol Merle and get on her waiting list."

Joy puts her hand on her forehead. "I'll go see Merle in person tomorrow! I got an idea I wanna ask her about. Alright," she stands at the head of the table, "we are all in place, everyone knows what they're supposed to do tomorrow? Cristal and Lexus, you got the route down? Otis and Leviticus, make sure you're listening to the buzz in the casino. There's only one thing left: we haven't responded to the Owners's request for a meeting yet, and I'll set up a time."

Anita stands. "All of y'all are making me so happy right now. I still can't believe I let y'all talk me into this mess, but it feels good."

Gerald gets up, walks around the table and hugs her. Everyone else looks at each other with soft eyes. Gerald turns to everyone, wiping his tears. "Let's eat before these oxtails get cold!"

July 13

Once upon a time across the bridge from Bowfin Street, past the dilapidated casino, and up into the hills, Cristal drives the bus under the curtain of darkness, down shifting and swinging the wide steering wheel through switchbacks. Charlene sits behind her. William Earl Townsend III and Delores the Artist sit behind them. Lexus lays on her back in the seat behind them with her eyes closed mumble-reciting the art information, P.E.S.T.S. she reminds herself which is an acronym she made up that means Project, Enunciate, Say That Shit. They are on their way to show the Owners the art in a soft opening of the tour before the official meeting.

Cristal continues to chug the bus upward until she reaches a flat outcrop and turns the engine and lights off. One side of the outcrop overlooks the twinkling lights of the rich people's homes all the way down to the glowing casino reflecting in the bay. On the other side, a sloping black, but in daylight weeds and rocks. Here they wait in silence until the dirty pink light spreads over the bay, inches up the hills.

"Let's do it," Cristal says, starting the engine. Lexus steadies herself by holding onto a plastic strap from the ceiling, moves to the side of Cristal. She rubs Cristal's shoulder and strokes her hair. Charlene moves to the middle seats, the best spot for her to hear all the talk. William Earl Townsend III and Delores the Artist tell Cristal, Lexus, and Charlene good luck, and then get off the bus.

Lexus sits, and Cristal pulls the bus down the hill. The first stop is in front of Lime-Green Velour Robe's house. She lays on the horn. Before she's finished, neighbors start to come out of their houses, eager. Lime-Green Velour Robe ambles out in his lime green velour robe, slumped and grumpy. Outside the gate is today's newspaper he scoops up after multiple attempts, the wind moving it further away each time. He loses his balance before grabbing it and shoving it into his robe's pocket.

Lime-Green Velour Robe strolls around to get on the bus, and before he steps up, he sees Willie Earl and Delores the Artist in the distance on the outcrop. Willie Earl in his suit waving stoically like a politician. Delores, in her black artist getup, stands with her arms crossed. She pulls her sunglasses to the tip of her nose and glares over the top. He puts two fingers in the air in acknowledgement, gets on the bus, and swipes his eye crust in the direction of Cristal. She feels sick, but musters a smile, says, "Good morning, sir, welcome to Townsend Touristiques."

Lexus chimes in, "Please have a seat, sir. We have a scrumptious tour in store for you today."

Willie Earl and Delores are running late to the appointment with the Owners. Willie Earl got ready at Gerald and Anita's. He has his custom-made suit on, shoes polished, he flicks the feather in his hat with his fingers, smooths out the tops of his pants and shakes the bottoms from getting tucked into his shoes. He sticks a toothpick in his mouth, and Auntie Anita takes it out of his mouth. "Don't be chewin on a damn toothpick when you talk to them folks, it's nasty," she says.

Willie Earl's laugh sits on top of the roof expanding like telephone wires, trying to touch the clouds. He's pacing the living room, which gives way to dancing across the floor, two-stepping and lifting his hands to the ceiling. "Come on now, Delores, get on over here, we got somewhere to be," he shouts out the window.

Across the street, Delores looks in the mirror one more time before leaving her apartment. Inconspicuous yet alluring she thinks to herself and laughs. "What babe says that kind of shit?" she says to the mirror. You do, that's who. Though they had agreed last night, she shouldn't talk in order to maintain an artist's mystique, let Willie Earl do all the talking.

She is sweating so much already and hasn't even made it all the way down the steps. Joy is in the entrance of the apartment building with a few maintenance women from the casino. She hands the women a crinkled, greasy paper bag. Delores overhears Joy saying, "Don't let them win too much or the casino will be suspicious." The maintenance women and Joy dap each other up, and the maintenance women leave, but not without looking over their shoulders first. Delores opens the door to go outside and Joy says, "See you later at the meeting!" while she runs upstairs. Once Delores is on the porch, she sees the art tour bus flash by in the distance, and it's so hot out the air is wavy.

She looks up to Uncle Gerald and Auntie Anita's and sees Willie Earl dancing in the front window. Superimposed over the window is the woman from yesterday. Now the woman is standing on their front porch. Her long dark hair is growing by the second. Delores starts walking faster, around the house to the back door, no way she's going to be caught up with this loony toon. She rounds the corner of the house to the backyard when two ropes of dark hair creep up behind her shoulders, wrap themselves around her chest. Delores starts to panic. "Get off me, babe," she says. But the hair continues to grow, twisting her into an embrace, starts pulsating to regulate Delores's breathing, and before she knows it, she realizes she is inhaling, exhaling deep and slow in time.

The hair turns her around, hugging her. Twenty-five feet away is the woman in the waders, and at her feet thousands of glistening cockle shells looking like gemstones in the sun. The woman in the waders smiles faintly, and nods her head toward Delores. "Oh hell naw!" Delores says, brushing the hair off. It falls quietly and disappears. She runs to the backyard, collapses on the stairs to the door, her hands grasping at her heart, trying to catch her breath again. She reaches down to her boot, and inside is a cockle shell.

Willie Earl's laugh bounds out of the door before he does and settles onto Delores's lap. "About time you got here, girl! Let's roll out!" Willie Earl says. "It's a fine day to get this money!"

In the hills, the bus tour is in full swing. Cristal has stopped and picked up every single one of the Owners and they do not sit next to each other, instead they each take up two or three seats, spreading their legs and bellowing loudly over each other about price points, savings and loans, and dividends. The Owners spit when they talk and gobs of white froth hang from the sides of their mouths. They all wear too-small or too-large aviator eyeglasses, their ties are too tight around their necks. They talk largely with their hands the louder their voices go. They fart and stick their fingers in their noses and then run their hands through their balding, slicked hair. The bus stops for the first time. Everyone is quiet.

Over the loudspeaker, Lexus says, "While we cannot permit you entry to the first exhibit, please allow me to introduce to you our first piece by the Artist. This is called "C'est Magnifique," made with five one-thousand-by-one-thousand . . ." Lexus begins but gets cut off by an Owner. "How the hell did she do it?" he says and the others mumble in agreement. They have arrived at an island no one on the bus recognizes with no entrance from the mainland.

Erect on the island is a life-size dollhouse in grayscale, the size of an actual house, with dusty windows that say Wash Me with a :(next to it. The left edge of the house has two-hundred-foot-tall silver hinges, as if the house can be opened, and if you squint your eyes and turn your head, the house looks slightly ajar.

"How much for this masterpiece?" an Owner asks. "We will pay top dollar! We will move it to the casino at once."

"Huzzah, hear hear!" says the rest of the Owners.

"This piece is not for sale," says Lexus. "Moving on . . ."

The Owners grumble and complain and curse under their breath. They begin to yell over top of one another about how everything has a price and everything can be bought and if they were going to go meet the artist anyway they should know what kind of deal they should be striking with her. Before they can get another word in, the hydraulics of the bus harrumph them to the next stop.

"Gentlemen," Lexus says, "If you would kindly draw your attention to your left windows, you will see exhibit number two." In the middle of a No Outlet street thousands of miniature panda bears no larger than three inches tall stacked in a cylinder shape go as far up to the sky as they can see, disappearing into the clouds, no end in sight. "The Artist calls this piece 'Ain't No Party Like a July Party,' and what is astonishing about this piece is that all the pandas move and eat and copulate and defecate and urinate in perfect symbiosis. Don't stand too closely!" The Owners watch as the panda bears shit on each other's heads and eat bamboo growing from the sky. They clumsily grope each other's backsides as they rock furiously, then more lazily. The Owners slam their heads into the glass of the bus windows to try to get a better look, all of their eyes moving toward the sky simultaneously.

"Please, sirs, take your seats, you do not want to miss the next one!" Lexus says. Cristal jerks into gear and the whole bus shudders. They are going to be late for the meeting but they must show them one more exhibit. As the bus winds around the bottom of the hills into town, Cristal starts getting nervous. The plan was she was going to really talk this one up, but the fog is so thick. She glances up into her mirrors and she can see Charlene and Lexus getting worried, too. The Owners now look bored, no longer talking to each other. Bald Spot 'n' Goatee is asleep with his big head fallen backward and his mouth gaping open snoring, which doesn't seem to bother the rest of them. Golden Chalice is pounding his fingers into a noisy calculator and saying, "No, no, the numbers don't add up," to no one in particular, sipping from his golden chalice. Shiny Shoes has taken his shoes off, which stink to high heaven, and is clipping his toenails. XXX is eating a limburger sandwich he has been carrying in his briefcase this entire time, the horrendous smell competing with the feet, and Lexus and Charlene are holding their noses and breathing through their mouths. Cristal dips her nose into the front of her shirt. Birthmark with the Gun keeps tapping on the glass of the window with his fingers, caressing the gun bulge on his side in rhythm. Lime-Green Velour Robe and Reflecting Mirror are both picking their noses but trying to act like they aren't. In the distance, Cristal sees the next exhibit cut through the fog.

"My esteemed guests, we are at our grand finale before you meet the Artist herself. We will park and open the doors for you to explore and interact with this next exhibit, surely to be the showstopper of your interest." They park in the empty industrial lot by the casino, which has the Owners pleased since they own the property already. One by one they push and knock each other over, banging each other on the head, tripping each other to get out of the bus to see up close what is glowing, overpowering the sun, dripping in dazzle.

What shines is an orchard, lines of tall, full-grown, majestically knotted and thick trunked trees made of twenty-four karat gold. On these trees, heavy digitized fruits hang, covered in SMPTE color bars buzzing as if staticky. The fruits glisten, moisture on the sides and gleaming, which makes the Owners hungry. The Owners begin salivating, pulling and stepping in front of, over, above one another to get a better look at the trees and their fruits. XXX yanks a drooping one from a branch, the fruit shocks him. He drops it, all the other Owners laugh. This angers XXX so much he picks up the fruit again, even though it is still shocking him, and throws the fruit at the tree. The tree begins to shake. Then the tree next to it begins to shake. Then the tree next to the two trees begins to shake. The entire orchard is shaking. The Owners push, pull, yank, throw elbows to faces to scramble back into the bus. Cristal, Lexus, Charlene laugh and laugh at them. They don't even bother sharing the name of the piece. The Owners start yelling again about prices, how much for these trees, we want them, the whole lot, we want every single one, and what are those buzzing colored foods hanging from the branches, how did she do it, it's marvelous, a wonder, brilliant, genius, a sensation!

Cristal turns on the microphone with some feedback and it stings everyone's ears with the sharp screech. "Thank you, sirs, for your attention. I hear you asking about prices, and of course, all of the pieces on exhibit are subjective to current competitive market prices concurrent with the art world-at-large, and, of course, at the discretion of the artist whether she wants to sell or not. These three pieces are only a few of the pieces in our fine city. Again, thank you for your time and attention. We will now be dropping you off at the amphitheater where you will meet William Earl Townsend III and the Artist. Please save further questions for your briefing. We thank you for your patronage, and your guestage."

As they drive to the amphitheater, Charlene asks "What's a guestage?" and Lexus shrugs.

Cristal pulls into the parking lot. The men are still shouting about prices until Lexus stares them down. Lexus says, "Thank you for your silence before entering such a sacred space. The Artist does not tolerate frivolous noise. If you feel you must speak to the Artist or William Earl Townsend III, please do so in an orderly fashion or there will be no meeting, no deals, and we will return you to your homes to await William Earl Townsend III and the Artist's legal decision. Please exit in a single file line, and keep walking single file, slowly, until you reach the bottom row of the amphitheater. Once there, you will sit next to each other, with your hands in your laps, in the order you exit this bus. I must reiterate, any outbursts or sudden movements, and the meeting will be over, OH-VERR."

Charlene and Lexus stand on each side of the door while bowing with one arm gesturing toward a red carpet lined with red velvet ropes leading to the amphitheater. The men file off and onto the carpet, which turns into an oval of orange under each footstep. They quietly ooh and ahh. Bald Spot 'n' Goatee says under his breath, "Townsend is a classy fellow!" As they get closer to the amphitheater, the same gold trees with heavy digitized fruit line each side of the red carpet, branches connecting to make a tunnel. The fruit refracts rainbow light onto the gold-branch tunnel walls, and the light keeps bouncing from fruit to wall to fruit to the oval orange carpet steps. Shiny Shoes waves his hand through the light, his fingers trying to grasp it, then he reaches higher to grab a fruit but Lexus says "Please refrain" and he stuffs his hand in his pocket and looks away whistling.

Once they exit the tree branch tunnel, they file into the semi-circular amphitheater and sit in the front row as instructed, quiet, hands in laps. Charlene stands at the end of the row. Lexus stands at the other end of the row.

They wait. They wait. Until William Earl Townsend III walks in from the right with his arms clasped behind his back. He surveys the men without saying a word, looks back in the direction from where he came and nods yes. Uncle Gerald, Joy, and Delores are off to the side, out of sight, listening. Delores the Artist walks out and stands next to Willie Earl. With two hands, she holds a digitized fruit in front of her belly, making her torso glow. Her sunglasses stare straight ahead. She doesn't say a word.

"Gentlemen," William Earl Townsend III says. "Welcome. I trust you have been informed of the guidelines for today's meeting. Please take a few minutes to silently designate one person amongst you who will speak for all of you."

They don't have to decide because Lime-Green Velour Robe always speaks for them, so to make a show of power like they have their shit together, they don't waste time deciding, and the Owner raises his hand.

William Earl Townsend III studies the man silently, and says, "Are you all sure this is your designated speaker?" They don't say anything, and the Owner keeps his hand raised. "Very well," William Earl Townsend III says and looks to Delores the Artist. "Does this suit you?" he asks. She nods. "We shall proceed," he says. "First order of business is to address the issue of you illegally profiting from my client's work, albeit on your property. Perhaps you were ignorant and may not have been acting maliciously, but now you are aware, and your ignorance will no longer be a viable excuse. We will require a further examination of your financial records to determine the exact dollar amount you have procured from said works of art."

Lime-Green Velour Robe stands to oppose and says, "Why would you need our financial records! Preposterous! Ludicrous!"

"This meeting is terminated. Good day, sirs," Willie Earl says, turning to leave the podium, nodding to Delores.

The Owners start to grumble in protest. Lime-Green Velour Robe says, "My apologies for the outburst! Excuse me! I think it's in our best interest we continue!"

Delores turns her back to the owners, smiles at Willie Earl, and slowly returns to the side of the podium, indicating the meeting will resume.

As Willie Earl takes his place back at the microphone, he says, "This is your last chance to abide by the guidelines. One more outburst and the deal is off the table." Willie Earl smooths his coat sleeves, adjusts his cufflinks, cracks his neck. He goes on, "Once we review your financial records, we can determine an appropriate percentage of the funds to allow you to retain, seeing that the works of art are indeed on your physical property, which isn't worth much according to my sources. If this requirement is not fulfilled, we will proceed toward litigation, which I assure you, will not be favorable for you. You may respond."

Lime-Green Velour Robe slowly raises his hand. "Yes, Mr. Townsend—"

"You may refer to me as William Earl Townsend III, nothing less, nothing more. Please continue."

"I'm sorry, William Earl Townsend III . . . I . . . we . . . agree with your requirements." He turns and winks at Shiny Shoes and XXX.

"Does this suit you?" he asks Delores the Artist. She nods.

"Our second order of business, since you agree with our requirements, is seeing as to how the public has adored my client's work on your property, undoubtedly making it more beautiful than perhaps it has ever been, we will allow you to keep the existing work on said property, and allow you to keep charging admission. Townsend Touristiques will see to it patrons are delivered to your property as part of the tours. However, this service is not free. Seeing as you have high-value art you did not purchase, added to the steady stream of patrons we will deliver to your doorstep, we will collect 50 percent of all revenue you earn from admission. You may respond."

Lime-Green Velour Robe does some quick math in his head and figures even giving away 50 percent with an increase of customers, he will still make more money than he currently is. Just as he's raising his hand, purple fog fills the amphitheater. The woman in the waders appears between Willie Earl and Delores and puts her arms around their shoulders.

Joy is whispering to Gerald, "That broad gonna fuck up this whole thing. Get her outta here."

Gerald whispers back, "How can I get her outta here, should I call her, hey ghost lady come here, we got some creepy shit over here for you in the cut."

Willie Earl and Delores try to keep their composure.

The Owner finishes raising his hand and says, "I agree to those terms and find them quite favorable for all involved."

Joy looks at Gerald and says, "The Owners can't even see the broad and all the dramatic-ass fog. She ain't scaring nobody."

"Does this suit you?" Willie Earl asks Delores the Artist, but she *is* scared of the lady in waders who is now gripping her shoulder hard, wondering if she should punch the babe or try to run because fuck a ghost. "Ma'am, I repeat, does this suit you?" he asks louder. Delores nods.

Lime-Green Velour Robe raises his hand again.

"You may speak," Willie Earl says.

"May we hear from the Artist herself about inspiration?" the Owner asks.

"No, you may not," Willie Earl says. The woman in waders pinches her right hand fingers and thumb together, kisses, and blows the kiss, indicating they are doing a good job. The owner raises his hand again.

"You may speak," Willie Earl says, "and you are permitted no further inquiries, so ensure that this last inquiry is of the utmost relevance to our business arrangement."

The Owner clears his throat and asks, "As a businessman like yourself, William Earl Townsend III, with an appreciation for business acumen, I admire what you all are doing here with tours and art, and I'm wondering if you'd be so kind to let us know the current and projected net worth of your business model?"

Willie Earl is reaching deep for his response. Joy told him to expect this question, but he didn't think they would ask, so he half-heartedly memorized an answer because he was memorizing too much already, changing his speech too much, putting on too many airs, being all high saditty, but after the woman pats his back again for what feels like encouragement, he finds his response: "That is, shall we say, none of your concern. I, too, can appreciate businessmen like myself who have an affinity for the subtle art of a well-planned business model guaranteed to thrive under the right leadership, so, from a like-mind to a like-mind, and as a professional courtesy, I will tell you my bus tour and my client's art is the future of Tannery Bay, because, as you and I are both well aware, businesses in this town have been on the decline for quite some time now. Unless your businesses are the exception? Thank you, gentlemen. Our driver and tour guides will return you to your places of residences."

The Owners stand, and Lexus and Charlene lead them out of the amphitheater single file, back onto the red carpet, through the tree branch tunnel, and onto the bus. On the bus, Lime-Green Velour Robe whispers to Shiny Shoes and XXX, "Oh, they will know soon enough how our businesses are quite the exception." The men chuckle.

Once the men leave the amphitheater, the woman in the waders removes her arms from Willie Earl and Delores's necks, Delores swatting at her and going through her like mist. The woman walks in front of them to face them, and raises her right fist. She looks over to Uncle Gerald and Joy, and raises her fist again. Then vanishes.

July 14

Once upon a time on Bowfin Street, the sky holds a pink hue unlike anything anyone in Tannery Bay has ever seen, an iridescent film like the top of the bay. People all over the neighborhood stop walking and drinking coffee and flipping Open signs on storefronts and talking to each other to look to the sky. The rainbow film swirls into the clouds and at the right angle casts a shadow of rainbow on the neighborhood where the children on the street chase a ball. Willie Earl sits on the stoop and watches the children chase the shadow.

Today is the first day of Townsend Touristiques that is open to the public, which the Owners announced immediately yesterday evening, of course, at a hefty price, which really means the public tour is only open to the rich folks from the Hills. They are gonna see some shit today, Willie Earl laughs to himself and the laugh leaves the stoop and floats like a dragonfly to the children, bounces on the ball, dances in the rainbow shadow. He puffs and blows out his cigar smoke. Whistles one of Anita's tunes low and slow. The smoke pulls itself to the middle of the street where the woman in the waders stands in the last bit of faint rainbow shadow.

"Can I help you? You done look like you need helped," Willie Earl says. She doesn't move. She doesn't even look like she's breathing. "You wanna come with me? You wanna see what these fools are gonna see?" and he reaches out his hand toward her. She does not move. "Well, if you're comin, come on," and he leaves the stoop and starts to walk. A half a block away, he looks back and she's trailing behind him. He smiles to himself and starts whistling again.

Across the bridge at the bottom of the hill, the bus, sparkling chrome glint in the sun, purrs in wait. Lexus takes the tickets as the bus fills. "Choose a seat folks, any seat, this isn't a wedding, there ain't no sides," she yells. Cristal is driving. She feels anxious today, more anxious than she was with the Owners. Auntie Anita has been hard at work, and this morning when she got back from being gone all night, she told them these rich folks have everything in store for them, which she wasn't sure about, no one has seen what Auntie Anita has been up to.

Lexus gets on the intercom. "We here at Townsend Touristiques want to extend the most heartfelt thank you and appreciation to all of you who support the Arts. As we move through each exhibit today, please do observe the guidelines of the Artist: do not touch unless told you may touch; do not cross the red lines unless explicitly ordered to do so; sign the following waiver."

At the last minute, Anita made the Owners force the rich folks to sign a waiver recusing Townsend Touristiques of any trouble because don't start no shit, there won't be no shit, Anita said and Willie Earl agreed. The rich folks did not delay, and did not ask any questions about the waiver. The only words Lexus could make out at a cursory glance was "not responsible for death," which she felt her brow furrow over. "Art is dangerous," she said to Cristal who only nodded because she didn't know what she was referring to.

Once all the waivers are collected, the tour starts. They drive for what feels like forever, and Cristal is the only one who knows where they are going because Anita is directing her through an earpiece. "No map," Anita said. "All the windows on the bus should be blacked out," she directed. "I don't want these fools knowin a goddamn thing."

The first stop is through the woods, down a long clearing that isn't actually a road at all. The bus begins to rock and sway under what seems to be soft ground, then mud, then huge puddles where the tires are barely getting through. "Keep on going," Anita says in Cristal's earpiece and she grips her hands at ten and two and keeps the bus steady. "Stop," Anita says. Cristal brakes, sending everyone crashing from their seats, spilling out onto the floor or smashed into the seat ahead of them. Everyone complains loudly, and Lexus gets on the intercom. "Thank you for your patience, folks. We have arrived to exhibit one. Please leave all of your belongings on the bus. Please, single file from the back of the bus," and then the hydraulics air out and shift, the back of the bus swings wide open. "Once out, please await further instruction."

While they were driving, the sky turned from pink to a light green. This is a light green that scares Cristal. She knows what this light green could mean.

Outside, Cristal walkie talkies to Lexus to line everyone up in the field in rows of two by two, one hundred feet apart. "Tell them to keep their hands at their sides, to take all jewelry and hats off, to put their hair up into a bun, to tuck their shirts in," Cristal says to Lexus. She watches Lexus wildly gesture with her arms and hands as she explains to each pair the instructions. Cristal starts to sweat, her palms are clammy and prickly, and no matter how much she wipes them on her jean shorts, they still stay drenched.

"Tell Lexus to get back into the bus immediately, but before she does, tell her to introduce the piece," Anita says to Cristal who relays the information to Lexus. Cristal can hear Lexus say to the final pair closest to the bus, "Thank you, everyone, for your cooperation. Please keep still and we will remind you that no photography or video is allowed. The exhibit will last only three minutes. This piece is called 'See You on the Flip Side.'"

Lexus runs and jumps into the bus, looking frazzled and excited. "Put on your earmuffs and your goggles," Anita says to Cristal and she instructs the other girls. Together they sit with orange ear protection and fogged blue-eyed goggles and wait. "See you on the flip," Anita says.

A whistle starts, long and loud, a chugging fills the space, the sky, the huge field, a chugging like the biggest train they have ever heard barreling toward them full speed. The windows begin to rattle, the bus begins to shake, the air outside the bus glowing a darker green. Cristal says, "Hold on to something!" and moves over to Lexus. They wrap their bodies around each other. "Here we go!" Lexus yells, and just as she yells, the sound stops. Everything goes silent. Everything is still.

Lexus sees them first, barreling down the one-hundred-foot spaces between pairs. Gray funnel clouds, gathering speed, out of nowhere. The bottoms are so skinny, barely contacting the ground. The winds so fast, so fierce and for one second she is afraid for the rich people. The tornadoes rip through the middle lanes without losing control. The girls can hear the people scream. The bus shakes so hard they think it will topple over. Cristal starts to laugh. Lexus starts to cry.

Just as fast as it starts, it stops. The tornados are gone. The sky is as pink as it ever was, no clouds.

Lexus can't calm down. Cristal hugs her, but thinks she needs to buck up if she's going to work here. Auntie Anita comes on in Cristal's ear. "Alright then, y'all go on out and gather those folks, bring 'em to the next spot." Dazed, Cristal motions to Lexus to open the door. Outside most of them are still standing, except in the front there are two missing, one from each pair. Up in the trees, they see one. Several of them have lost wigs. Several of them have lost shirts or shoes.

When they file back onto the bus, everyone is silent. Lexus gathers herself, "We hope you enjoyed "See You on the Flip Side." Please sit back and enjoy the ride. We will be at exhibit number two in no time."

Cristal bounces the bus back out of the woods. Everyone is still shook, glancing out the windows looking for more tornadoes. At the slightest wind rustled tree branch, they grab the back of the seat in front of them and brace. On top of the bus, the woman in waders sits with her legs dangling over the side. The bus lurches back onto asphalt, and Cristal swings the wheel to head back toward town. Anita in the earpiece says, "Y'all know what to do next—me and Gerald gonna take Cora Mae out to blow some bubbles and play hopscotch with the other babies. See y'all when you get back. Good job, Cristal and Lexus."

Lexus places her hand on Cristal's neck and lightly touches it. "You're doing good." The warmth from Lexus's hand spreads throughout Cristal's body and she breathes relief. She sees Lexus smiling in the rearview mirror.

Approaching town, they pass the fishery and pull into the police station's front parking lot. The back of the police station faces the bay. "Don't worry," Lexus says, standing. "We're not putting you all in jail. Our next exhibit, entitled 'Le Soirée,' is on the old access road behind the police station." Lexus walks up the aisle and gives everyone a faded yellow cone party hat with a black veil attached to the front. She walks back to the front. "Please put on your hat-veil before exiting."

The stench of the bay hits first, and then the fog soaking up the dirty pink light. Lexus and Cristal lead the group through the parking lot and around the police station to the old access road. The old access road is asphalt cracked like a jigsaw puzzle with tufts of dead grass poking through. Painted yellow footsteps lead to the wide wooden dock, faded and leaning out into the bay. On each side of the dock entrance, sitting on waist-high stacks of cinderblocks, are two phonographs with brass flaring horns that bloom like flowers. Wobbly records play a skipping, deep voiced static loop of:

Lollipop lollipop
Oh lolli lolli lolli

After they file onto the dock, they see a row of three open and two closed black caskets facing the bay like they are marching off into the water.

Casket One: [opened] filled with the purple bay water bubbling. Smiling rubber ducks float and bump into each other.

Casket Two: [opened] filled with the purple bay water surrounding a miniature model of Tannery Bay, flooded halfway up to the casino. The Hills are safe.

Casket Three: [opened] Behind the casket is a table with stacks of fine china bowls. Each person is instructed to pick up a bowl and soup spoon. Large ladles hang over the edge of the casket. Hot purple bay water bubbling and steaming, casino chips and cockle shells floating. A white sign on the inside the length of the opened lid says: All You Can Eat.

Casket Four: [closed]

Casket Five: [closed]

The people plead to know what's in the caskets. Lexus tells them to imagine. They keep pleading. Cristal tells them their worst fears are in there. They try to open the caskets but can't. They keep taking turns, teamwork, fingers on every inch of the casket lid prying and prying and grunting and prying and grunting. They throw their bowls and spoons at it, but they all ting off and fall into the bay, the gel-water sucking them down. Nothing.

They walk single file back to the bus defeated, but invigorated. Their yellow party hats tilted to the sides, black veils sticking to their sweaty faces. Once everyone is back on the bus and Cristal is driving away, the caskets start to creak open, Willie Earl's laugh faintly rising from Casket Four.

July 15

Once upon a time across the bay from the old fishery and the police station, Auntie Anita stands on the dock behind Gerald's old juke joint, looking across to the blip of caskets on the police station dock. Next to the dock looms the old fishery with its faded wooden planks and three industrial cranes stretch angled to the sky like brontosaurus necks, rusted pulleys at the top, tattered ropes dangling.

Auntie Anita ain't been in the fishery or the juke joint since they shut it down. She had wanted to go but couldn't bring herself to. Last night the woman in waders sat at her kitchen table pointing to the juke joint. Anita shook her head no, but the woman kept pointing.

Here is Anita in this early pink light, turning to walk into the back door of the juke joint. Inside, light beams through the holes in the roof and filters through the cracks of the wooden floor planks until the black of the basement absorbs it. The bar is still intact, and she remembers Gerald behind it with a white towel flung over his left shoulder, pouring his hooch into a row of ten shot glasses.

She sits at the wooden table in front of the bar, in the exact chair she was sitting in when they were about to shut it down for good all those Julys ago. Eight-year-old Otis sat across from her. Gerald was to her right, and eight-year-old Joy sat across from him. They were waiting for Otis and Joy's parents to come back from across the bay, making one last delivery of hooch to the fishery. They were eating hush puppies and honey for breakfast and playing spades. Otis and Anita were winning, and at that moment,

Otis was the loud one and Joy was the quiet one, so Otis was talking shit and slamming the cards down.

Anita said, "Go head, baby! Gerald's lil punk-ass queen can't do shit!"

Then Joy slid her card nicely face down like it was an accident, and when Otis flipped the card over, they all saw it was a big joker. Gerald jumped up from the table and high-fived Joy, and Joy stuck her tongue out at Otis, and said, "That's what you get for talking shit."

In the middle of Gerald and Joy celebrating, Good Ol Pearl Anne ran through the back door, couldn't speak, choking on her crying.

Anita and Good Ol Pearl Anne were supposed to make a last run across the bay but they wanted to help Gerald finish cleaning out the juke joint, so Anita's sister Betty Lee and her old man Woodrow said they'd make the run. They'd done it a few times before. Because this was the last run, they loaded up a lot of cases of hooch onto Pearl Anne's contraption and let them hang below the boat as usual. The boat sat a little lower because of the weight, and floated a little slower.

On the way to the fishery, Betty Lee and Woodrow talked about having a big surprise party for Otis and Joy, wanting them to experience a special birthday for once.

Betty Lee said, "We can have the party right at the juke joint."

Woodrow said, "Yes yes! And we can get Slack-String Jones to play his stand-up bass, we can get Crazy-Leg Carl to dance, Fish-Lips Larry on the trumpet, and I'll be on the sticks!"

Betty Lee, letting her fingers glide through the water. She said, "Oooh yes, and me and Anita will sing. We gonna throw the biggest soirée in the bay!" They continued rowing, making plans in excited whispers, what type of food, all the gifts they were gonna buy, all the neighborhood children they were gonna invite.

Betty Lee and Woodrow docked the boat on the back side of the fishery like usual, quietly unloaded the hooch, and quietly stashed it in the secret floor door at the bottom of the fishery, but like unusual, two cops were laying in the dark on their bellies on their dock, covered with black blankets. When Betty Lee and Woodrow got back in the boat and started across the bay, the two cops hopped down into their own boat and followed.

Good Ol Pearl Anne was standing on the dock in the early light, waiting for them to show up. She was squinting her eyes at the boat as it bobbed up to the dock. Bullet holes and blood. No bodies. She walked through the back door, leaned against the frame, and when Anita called for her, she slumped to the floor. The bodies were never found. At the funeral were two closed caskets.

Anita comes out of her memory crying, and doesn't know why she's standing in the doorframe instead of sitting like she was when she first started remembering. The light is no longer beaming through the holes in the roof because it's dark now. She looks at the table, and in the chairs sit concrete replicas of eight-year-old Otis and Joy, young Gerald, and young Anita as they were back then playing cards. She sees the bliss in all of their faces.

She looks toward the bar and sees the woman in waders pouring Gerald's hooch into shot glasses, cockle shells in the bottoms. Anita walks over to the woman, who points to the glasses, and Anita picks up one, the woman picks up one, and they clank glasses and shoot the hooch. Then a second one. And a third. The woman vanishes. Anita counts the glasses, thirty-seven, then walks home with the bottle of Gerald's hooch.

Later, in bed, while Gerald watches *The Flip Wilson Show*, Anita pulls out the bottle of hooch from under her pillow and hands it to him without looking at him.

"Well, what do we have here? I thought there was no hooch left," Gerald says, laughing, pushing his glasses up on to his head, squinting his eyes, turning the bottle over and over again in his hands. "Anita, you been to the juke joint! I thought . . ."

"Hush about it."

"Well alright now," Gerald says as he pops the cork and swirls it under his nose before he dips the whole bottle back and takes a drink. "Ahhh," he laughs again in satisfaction. He tips the bottle to Anita, who waves her hand in refusal. "You sure?" he teases, and her glare is enough to say yes she is sure.

Gerald recorks the bottle and puts it on his nightstand. "Say, are you not gonna head out tonight?" He turns to face her and drapes his arm around her.

"No," she says as she closes her eyes, "I've done enough work for today." She leans down and kisses his shoulder and then his forehead.

Anita wakes up in the same position she fell asleep in, Gerald's arm draped around her body, the TV soft and staticky. She's restless, and decides to head out into the streets anyway, even though she told Gerald she was staying in. She feels rested and ready, her head filled with installation ideas as she gets up and around, makes a pot of coffee, packs her knapsack up with supplies. Once outside, the pink air feels light and cool against her cheekbones and she walks across the bay bridge in the motionless darkness, humming her song into the water below. Coming off the bridge, she notices Rashaad's Reliable Junkyard truck parked on the street, and

July 16

Once upon a time across the bridge from Bowfin Street, behind the dilapidated casino, at the bottom of the Hills, Lexus waits, straddling her bike, feet solid to the ground, jaw clenched. Today is Lexus's day off the bus tour because she is being initiated into the Queers on Gears. Her whole life she knew one day she would be a part of the Queers on Gears. She would see those daddy dykes and those butch dykes and those femme dykes dredging across the bridge in groups coming home from the tannery or the casino, sitting on the edge of turned over five gallon buckets fishing, hanging out outside the package store, the convenience store, the grocery store.

They volunteered their time getting meals to shut-in folks. They ran the soccer program practices and you would see them out there with their whistles around their necks shouting at the kids "good job!" and "play like a team!" and "give me ten squat thrusts!" and it made Lexus laugh right now, thinking about Delores and her damn squat thrusts as a punishment for screwing around and not running the soccer drills. Lexus remembered during a soccer practice she was temporarily in love with her friend Destiny. Lexus was always falling in temporary love. Instead of running the ball to the goalie as instructed by Delores, she went to the overgrown field next to the soccer field and picked a bouquet of wildflowers for Destiny. Lexus could hear Delores yelling "Lexus, ten squat thrusts pah-leaze!" before she even turned around to come back. Made her lose her courage, she left the flowers with an agreement with herself to come back and give them to Destiny. She never did.

The kind of girl I am, Lexus thinks, is a girl who would rather pick flowers for the girl she loves than play soccer in the damn heat. Still, nope to a soccer game, I'm going to get my girl to love me. Something to be said for that, she thinks to herself.

Watching the Queers on Gears gave her what she needed to keep going. It was her greatest aspiration. She wanted to look like them, do good like them, be a part of a family like them. And now is her chance.

Yesterday after Cristal and Lexus dropped off the weary, wide-eyed rich folks from the coffin exhibit and were parking the bus for the night at Rashaad's, Delores slipped Lexus a piece of paper, folded into the shape of a star. Lexus was too keyed up to read it then, she just nodded at Delores and walked with Cristal back to Uncle Gerald and Auntie Anita's. She wanted to drop to her knees right there and tell Cristal how much she loved her, how her love is real and true, but she couldn't yet. She wanted to be made into the Queers on Gears before she let her feelings be known. She shook her head, she knew how silly it all was, but she wanted Cristal to really be proud of her, to know she had accomplished something great, she was finally going to belong to something good. The piece of paper said, "Meet at the bottom of the south side of the Hills at eleven a.m. tomorrow—don't be late."

She can see in the distance the mass of bikes and her palms start sweating. Today she will have to race Sweetheart, the baddest daddy of them all, up the mountain to the first ridge. The rumor is this is not a shoo-in situation, there have been people who have tried to beat her and failed, and not only people who want into the Queers on Gears. All kinds of folks have tried to beat her. She is a legend.

Up comes red bike after red bike, slick and twinkling in the hill fog, lined up and kicking dust in front of Lexus. There is

Rosalinda, front and center, who nods at Lexus and smiles. Another person down the line cracks their knuckles like this is a fight. Lexus tries not to laugh.

The middle of the line parts and in pedals Sweetheart, short and boxy with the softest face, the kindest eyes, fresh new fade, thin gold chain bouncing.

"Line 'em up!" Rosalinda yells and sounds the air horn to which the rest of the line reacts in a mix of covering their ears, scowling, and laughing in anticipation.

Sweetheart shuffles her bike to the starting line a few feet away from Lexus. Lexus starts to sweat, every part of her. Sweetheart is so close. How will she ever beat her? She can smell her cologne, cedar and amber undertones mixed with sunshine and leather. Lexus feels intoxicated. She's ready.

Rosalinda steps in front of them and recites the following with her eyes closed: "Cheers queers, we are gathered here today as the order of Queers on Gears to welcome our sister Lexus. The grounds for being made are simple but not easy: You must beat Sweetheart in a hill race. If you beat her time, you are made. Once made, you are with us for life. There are hydration stations set up along the path—but be careful, you are being watched and timed accordingly. Are you ready?"

Sweetheart and Lexus look straight ahead, nod their heads yes.

"On your mark," and Rosalinda lifts the air horn into the air, "Get set," and Lexus puts one foot on her pedals, "Go!" and the air horn sounds.

Lexus pedals like her life depends on it. She does not look back at her opponent. She does not see when Sweetheart waits thirty seconds to give her the lead. Sweetheart takes off yelling,

"I'm coming for you, Lexus!" All the queers behind them are hooting and hollering in excitement and encouragement.

Lexus is standing up and pumping the pedals, leaning hard into the inside of the first switchback, tires spinning gravel, head down, pumping pumping pumping. She hears Sweetheart's tires crunching. Focus, focus, eyes on the road, she thinks, the words timed with her breath, focus, focus, eyes on the road.

The next switchback is a little far, and it's the first hydration station. Lexus sees a group holding out cups and cheering. She glances back and there's Sweetheart about three bike-lengths behind, creeping up on her back right. Lexus swings in front of Sweetheart, then Sweetheart switches lanes, and Lexus swings back in front of Sweetheart.

Lexus approaches the hydration station. Auntie Anita, Uncle Gerald, Otis, Leviticus, Joy, Cora Mae, Charlene, and Willie Earl are yelling GO, GO, GO! Cristal holds out a paper cup. Lexus swings over and grabs the cup with her right hand and chugs it, still pedaling, but Sweetheart leans hard on the inside of the switchback and takes the lead. Lexus crushes the paper cup and tosses it into a large trash can, puts her head down and pumps harder.

At the next switchback, Sweetheart swerves over to get water, and Lexus takes the lead by skidding through the turn and peeling out on the straight away toward the finish line. Sweetheart catches up, pulling up next to Lexus, neck and neck. Lexus puts her head down and pedals as hard as she can. Sweetheart pedals faster. Lexus pedals faster. People are at the finish line cheering. Neck and neck. Lexus digs deep into herself and gives one last push. Sweetheart eases up intentionally and Lexus crosses the finish line with a full bike-length lead. She drops her bike and lays on her back with her hands covering her face, panting. Sweetheart stands over her and says, "Congratulations, Lexus! You're made! You're made!" The crowd cheers while Sweetheart pulls Lexus to her feet and gives her some water.

Everyone else is walking up the hill to see who won, though the celebration is a dead giveaway. Cristal is leading the pack in a half jog. She sees Sweetheart holding up Lexus's arm, a champion. Cristal sticks two fingers into her own mouth and pierces a whistle through everyone else's cheers. Lexus waves "I'm in! I'm made!" Cristal reaches Lexus and they hug hard and long, burying their faces in each other's necks. Cristal kisses Lexus on the face, which makes Lexus blush, not from embarrassment, but from love.

Sweetheart points Lexus to what she calls the ceremonial grounds at the top of the ridge. Two horseshoe pits overlook the hill and into the bay. Smoke pours from the holes in the top of grills. Picnic tables form a large square. In the middle of the square on its own table sits a three—tiered cake in the shape of a spiral, little red candy bikes moving upward on white frosting with black piping. On the top of the cake is a figurine of Lexus on the classic red Queers on Gears bicycle.

Lexus can't believe it, all this for her. She stands straighter and smiles the biggest smile she's ever smiled in her smiling life.

Delores leads Lexus to the middle of the square. Delores hushes everyone and says, "Before we get to food and cake, we have something for you, Lexus." Sweetheart rolls out a new red bike. She says, "It's official! Welcome to the family!" Cristal cheers the loudest. Charlene has her hand on Cristal's back smiling to no end. Lexus soaks it all in, everyone cheering, everyone there to celebrate her, and lands on where she wants to be: Cristal's eyes. And for a few seconds, that's all that matters.

July 17

Once upon a time on Bowfin Street, Auntie Anita's been busy. After the Queers on Gears race, she and Uncle Gerald savored their walk home hand in hand, through the purple fog, watching the white smoke from the tannery fill the sky, sun seeping through the film, a painting all on its own. They see Rashaad loading up bags of clay into the back of his truck.

"Y'all headed back down to the sewer tonight?" Anita says.

Rashaad pats the bag of clay, "Yes ma'am."

Uncle Gerald says, "We're goin on a walk so I'll be back around to help you."

These are the moments Auntie Anita loves the most, when she decides everything around her is the most beautiful and she shares it with her man, who makes her laugh—downright holler sometimes—from the deepest part of her body. She jokes with him the only reason she's kept him around all these years is the way he makes her laugh. The way he makes everyone laugh. The way he makes everyone feel like they are the most important person in the world.

Another reason in the long list of reasons she loves Gerald, he is a man of boundaries. "The warrior in the garden," he tells her, an old Bruce Lee quote. "Better to be a warrior in the garden than a gardener in the war." But what the quote is missing, Anita thinks as she packs up her brushes and paints and blowtorch and pipes, is the fact that gardeners do their fair share of destruction—pruning, pulling, digging, ripping. Gardeners know how to fight and to finesse, how to design for the battle, how to prepare, how to be patient. After the walk, once Gerald leaves to help Rashaad, she looks around the living room one final time to make sure she has everything she needs. She is heading out to the old docks behind the juke joint no one uses except her neighborhood. She's putting the finishing touches on a piece everyone will love.

How anyone near the docks or who works on the docks or who boats daily didn't see what Anita was up to for nights upon nights is a testament to how bogged down everyone is these days, she thinks. She worked stealthily, sure, as to not be noticed, but certainly as the metal railings went up and the structure was being built, there had got to be someone curious? She laughs to herself, I guess not, though, everyone just minds their own business.

She comes back from the docks early and waits, makes herself a nice squat glass of ice tea in a mason jar, cleans herself up a little, scrubbing the dirt off her arms, a bit on her nails, changes her shirt, sits herself on the front porch in her rocking chair and watches the boys play basketball in the street, the girls doing each other's hair, waits for the newspaper to arrive.

She waves at a neighbor who yells "How you doin Auntie Anita?" and she says back "Oh, real fine, real fine. I saw your mama the other day, remember me to her, would you?" and he yells back "Yes, ma'am, sure thing. Nice to see you!" She folds her hands on her lap, looks at the pink sky and thinks, this July is all right, here in this one time, it is all right.

Down by the docks, people gather around the metal structure, beaming with lights across the bay, into people's boats, into the sky, beams of silver and gold and copper. The structure looks like a metal greenhouse of light, with no roof, and solid doors on either end. On the outside walls wheat paint murals of various scenes of the boys playing basketball on the street, the girls doing each other's hair, Charlene walking around with her crop top and cigarette, Otis and Joy sitting on the stoop across the way, Lexus and Cristal holding hands, and Willie Earl in his finest suit from the haberdashery looking so slick, my goodness. Beyond are the neighbors, and beyond that the docks, and beyond that the juke joint which is lit up with copper and gold and silver lights like the old days, big bass sounds of the most heavenly music coming from inside. Over the bay is Willie Earl's laugh dancing the two-step.

One of the old fishermen opens the door to the structure, and inside the structure is a flourishing garden full of foods, half a football field wide. Huge trees, lush vegetables and fruit plants, rows and rows of herbs and edible flowers. Everything bright and winking. A sign painted in bright calligraphy says "Eat What You Want. Take What You Want. Enough for Errybody."

The old fisherman takes his hat off his head and holds it to his chest. He sticks his head out of the door and says, "Y'all got to see this." Everyone walks in and the old fisherman stands there welcoming and speaking to them like it's his job. After the last person walks in, he puts his hat back on and talks to everyone, waving and smiling. Everyone is picking fruits and vegetables, talking about who is painted on the outside of the building, talking about making potato and leek stew, minestrone, cassoulet, collard greens with fatback, fruit salad with mint, caprese. Talking about the bike race yesterday, talking about how big the kids are getting, telling each other how good they look, inviting each other over for dinner tonight and tomorrow and the day after.

The old fisherman starts walking to the back, running his fingertips along the lush leaves, feeling like he's frolicking, and thinking, why haven't I frolicked in so long? At the back in a corner, on a table, he sees a small wooden box containing what looks like . . . no way it couldn't be, he thinks. He keeps getting closer as the contents of the box comes into focus, his throat tightens and his cheeks get hot: cockle shells. He grabs the box and runs out as fast as an old man can, headed to Auntie Anita's house.

Gerald returns, and he and Auntie Anita are on the front porch in their rocking chairs. Uncle Gerald asks about the hooch again, wondering where the ghost lady got it from. "Anita, I'm tellin' you," he says. "There was no more hooch left in the juke joint—Betty Lee and Woodrow carried the last bit of it across the bay to that goddamn fishery."

Auntie Anita rubs her chin, "Hmm . . ."

Uncle Gerald says, "I don't know either, maybe ghost lady try-na tell you you should go to the fishery."

"Me?" Auntie Anita says. "You mean Us, Gerald, Us." They both have vowed to never ever ever, *ever*, go to the fishery, knowing nothing can make them go, not even a ghost, but there's an unspoken softness and uncertainty in their eyes that says maybe they have to go. Just as they are about to come out of their silence, they hear "Anita! Anita!" and see the old fisherman running up the street with the wooden box cradled to his chest.

Panting, the old fisherman sits the box on the porch and puts one leg up and leans his elbow on his knee. "Anita, where did you get these? Do you know what they are?"

"Seashells?" Auntie Anita says.

"Nope," he says. "These ain't just any old seashells, these are *cockle shells*. Where you get 'em from?"

Auntie Anita looks at Uncle Gerald like, do I tell him? Uncle Gerald raises his eyebrows like, why not?

"Alright, Mr. Newbill," Auntie Anita says, "to put it plainly, a ghost woman has been giving them to us."

Mr. Newbill takes his hat off again and places it on his knee. "I have never seen these in real life, these cockle shells. The only reason I even know about 'em is because when I was a child, my grandpa, who was a fisherman, too, told me about 'em. He was obsessed with them. He was always sketching 'em. I have old notebooks upon notebooks filled with his sketches of these shells. He'd draw them on anything he could. Even carved bars of soap into the shape. Aw hell, his last words were talkin about 'em! We were always told not to speak of his obsession with these shells outside of the house, people would think he was crazy, and I actually thought he was crazy myself, but I wondered if there was something there, like a memory he couldn't quite get to. Forgive me grandpa, I'm so sorry. But here they are, real. Was my grandpa the ghost?"

"Naw," Anita says. "The ghost is a woman with tan waders on, or maybe it is your grandpa, he was a fisherman, who knows how the dead choose to be seen? If he was so obsessed with them, then maybe he's the one giving them to us, but why?"

"I don't know," Mr. Newbill says. "I really don't know, maybe it is him. I hope he visits me. But I need to go home and get myself together, look through the old notebooks, try to get my old mind to remember every last story he told me."

Mr. Newbill picks up a shell, rubs his fingers over the brown outer ridges, then swirls a finger around the smooth inside like cleaning out an ear. He holds it in front of his face examining it, then puts it to his ear and listens to the static swish of the bay. He says. "Would you mind terribly if I took one of these?"

Auntie Anita stands. "Mr. Newbill, you can have the whole box, we ain't got no use for 'em, and they really mean something to you. Please, take the whole box. And if we get more, I will make sure to scoot my ass right on over to your place and give 'em to you."

Mr. Newbill says, "Thank you, Anita, you surely are a blessing. Oh, and forgive my bad manners, thank you for the bounty, the food and the art."

"You're welcome, but it's y'all I should be thanking, seeing lives lived in this foul place keeps me going."

Mr. Newbill walks away cradling the box of cockle shells to his chest.

Uncle Gerald stands and hugs Auntie Anita, looks in her eyes and says, "Well sugarfoot, I guess we know what we gotta do now.

"I ain't going."

"It's the last place the hooch was," Gerald says. "Now we got a ghost fisherwoman and a live fisherman talkin bout these shells. It makes sense—I don't know what kinda sense it makes, but it's some type of sense—we gotta go to the fishery."

"I'm not ready."

"Me either."

July 18

Once upon a time across the bridge from Bowfin Street, past the dilapidated casino, and up into the hills at the edge of the forest, the bus lets out the softest cough into the air and then hums itself into a slightly louder song. Cristal and Lexus kiss on the bus when all the rich people are at each exhibit, sit on each other's laps in the driver's seat.

No wind in the trees this morning, the pink hue to the cumulus clouds big and fat look like they are going to eat them up. Cristal wouldn't mind, living in the sky on a fat pink cloud with Lexus for the rest of her days. She crunches the schedule of the day on her lap where she is drawing hearts with I love Lexus in cursive when Lexus looks into the rearview and says "What are you drawing?" Cristal freezes, tears the edge off the paper, and shoves it in her mouth. The ink tastes dusty, the way Auntie Anita's old trunks of paints smell, and she chews and chews fast until the paper is a hard wad.

Lexus laughs and shakes her head, "You didn't really want me to see, did you?" and Cristal flips her sunglasses down on her eyes, keeps chewing, rolling I Love You Lexus in red ink and hearts around on her molars. As she swallows hard, she thinks, maybe this will give me courage, give me strength, divine goddess. She says those words often to herself, please divine goddess help, though she doesn't exactly believe in anything, or maybe she believes in love, which is true, it was love at first sight with Lexus. The idea of the divine goddess has always been inside Cristal. Maybe it's the mother she has always been waiting for, always wanted, the one who will take care of her. The bus hits a bump sending her legs and arms spilling over the seat next to her. Lexus brakes, the hydraulics easing into their puff and rest. "We're here," Lexus says. "You can stop eating all the paper."

After they gather all the rich people for the day's activities, go through the Welcome and Keep Your Hands to Yourself spiel, they arrive at the first exhibit of the day. As they lead everyone off the bus, Lexus leans into Cristal's ear and says, "Get ready, Auntie Anita told me this is a doozy." Her breath grazing her ear sends goose bumps down Cristal's arms to her wrists.

They are in the middle of the forest situated on a dirt road disappearing into the horizon of the rolling green hills ahead. Nothing but thick pine trees and vibrant oaks with glowing magnolias shedding their head-sized blossoms to the ground.

"Please sit at the assigned seat according to the number you were given when you signed up for the tour. If you do not remember your number, one will be assigned to you after everyone has found their seats," Lexus says. So far they are having no problems because there is always at least one old dude who doesn't listen to instructions, doesn't have what he needs, forces one of the girls to do his bidding the entire day. But not today. Both girls look at each other with relief. "Please buckle your seatbelts. Fold your hands on your lap. Cross your ankles. Once the exhibit begins, please do not reach your hands or feet outside of your seat. Do not touch anything. You have been warned."

Lexus and Cristal go back into the bus and close the door. Lexus takes the driver's seat and Cristal climbs in her lap. No one fidgets or talks. This is a new exhibit and they want to watch. They will make out at the tornadoes.

The quiet is violently interrupted with dead magnolia blossoms suspended in the air. Lexus sees one go up and points out the window. Then another. And another. Soon fifteen magnolia blossoms are suspended in the air, glowing white and green, petals turning like a holy lotus. The magnolia blossoms expand in the sky, growing bigger and bigger, until they are the size of a man-size rainbow trout. The blossoms float daintily over to each person and land at their feet, emitting a silver glitter all over everyone's clothing, the chair, the dirt. The blossoms lay their petals down, animated like a human.

"Is that it?" Lexus says. "That's nothing."

"Shhh . . ." Cristal says. "Just wait."

They hear someone boo hiss and yell they want their money back when the magnolia blossoms come alive again, suspend in the air, turn themselves upside down, and hover above each person. They begin to lower themselves, enveloping each person into itself like a Venus flytrap, and as the petals completely fold in, both Lexus and Cristal see a flash of teeth, a wink of an eye from inside the carpel and stamen.

Neither Lexus nor Cristal reminds each other of the dogwood tree down the dirt road and into the clearing where they had carved their names the first time they ever hung out. Lexus loved Cristal's crooked front teeth and the way she lisped. She loved how kind she was, how much she loved her friends, how she was willing to do anything to bring a smile to other people. She was the only other girl who had a skateboard, too.

The first time they hung out was in this exact forest, with a group of friends around a campfire, too cold and windy to have a fire on the bay. Lexus was in love with Destiny, but she was also falling in and out of love so often it was hard for anyone to keep track. She was well—known around Tannery Bay for chasing after one girl or another, not that there was anything wrong with that, but not something Cristal was looking for. They ended up sitting next to each other, passing a bottle of TB Brew and sharing a blanket. The dogwood tree near them seemed to move closer with every pull from the bottle, until finally it was behind them, their backs resting against the large trunk. When the bottle was done, the fire roaring, Cristal pulled out a switchblade from her back pocket and turned to the dogwood, standing on the tree stumps they were sitting on, and carved L + C 4ever with a crooked heart around it like her teeth. The dogwood smiled at them, elongating its trunk even further, so the heart of the heart of the tree was resting deep within its chest, out of sight of everyone but them, their secret. "You want to be with me forever?" Lexus asked. This is the dilemma between them: Cristal never knows Lexus's true feelings or who she is in love with or if there is room for Cristal in her life.

At the tornado exhibit, the rich people look a little worse for wear. Cristal and Lexus are lounging on the back seats of the bus, Cristal picking at the skin on her nails and trying to hide the bleeding from Lexus by shoving her thumb into her mouth as fast as she can.

"You still with Whatsername?" Cristal asks. Cristal saw them together the other day, dipping their toes into the Bay, purple film on their feet.

Lexus shrugs. The bus shakes with the impending tornado, the sky green and mean. This is always the worst part of the exhibit. Cristal lays down on the seats and buries her face into Lexus's stomach. "I don't want you to be," she says, but Lexus doesn't hear her over the fierceness of the wind.

July 19

Once upon a time across the bay from the juke joint, Uncle Gerald and Auntie Anita had walked across Bay Bridge, past the dilapidated casino, past the tannery, past the police station, and stood holding hands in front of the old fishery.

"You ready?" Uncle Gerald says.

"Ready as I'll ever be," Auntie Anita says.

"Yeah, me either," Uncle Gerald says, dropping his hand and his head.

"Me either," Auntie Anita says, kicking some dust.

"We some chumps, we got weak in our old age."

"You're alright, Gerald, I'm the one who got weak."

Uncle Gerald agrees. They grab each other's hands again and start the walk back to Bowfin Street.

Once they get to the middle of the bridge they can see the juke joint, and the same memory plays in both their heads at the same time:

The band at the juke joint is in their groove. Slack-String Jones thumping the stand-up bass, Fish-Lips Larry piercing sharp notes on the trumpet, Sweet-Phalanges Phil gliding up and down the piano. Woodrow drumming a kick, snare, kick and high hat: boom, tap, boom and high tap.

The floorboards are bouncing under dancing feet, rattling bottles of hot sauce and malt vinegar off the tables. Child Otis, Joy, and Charlene run to catch them before they shatter on the floor. Anita and Betty Lee are on stage smiling while singing, "Shake that shuga shuga to the left . . . Shake that shuga shuga to the right," while looking at Gerald behind the bar with that same white towel over his left shoulder.

Anita and Betty Lee are keeping up with the tempo, like usual, when Anita slows into a low OOOOOOOH, and everyone stops dancing. Betty Lee and the band look confused for a slight second, and all the music drops, except for Slack-String's stand-up bass that now matches Anita's tempo. OOOOOOOH. A hot sauce bottle stops in midair above Joy's open hands. A malt vinegar bottle stops in mid air above Charlene's open hands. Gerald is pouring Willie Earl a drink and the hooch stops midair, mid-pour. Willie Earl stops talking midsentence, his mouth wide and his finger pointing to the sky. Anita is singing directly to Gerald, a fragmented melody that came to her that morning:

OooOOooOOOOHhhh

I don't CARE what they SAAAAY

sumthin's at the bottom of the BAAAAY

She looks away from Gerald and goes right back into "Shake that Shuga," but only the slow bass is playing. The rest of the band looks at each other and shrugs, picks it back up swinging. People start dancing again. The hooch resumes falling into Willie Earl's glass. The hot sauce bottle falls into Joy's hands. The malt vinegar bottle falls into Charlene's hands.

The memory releases Uncle Gerald and Auntie Anita, who are still halfway across the bridge facing each other. They tilt their heads to the side in bewilderment, realizing in their silence they had the same memory.

"Did you . . ." Auntie Anita says.

"Did you . . ." Uncle Gerald says.

"I don't remember," Auntie Anita says.

"I kinda remember," Uncle Gerald says. They don't know what

else to say, so they keep walking across the bridge and into the graveyard. The woman in waders starts to float over to them but Auntie Anita holds her hand up and says, "Un-unh, not today." The woman vanishes.

Auntie Anita and Uncle Gerald make it through the graveyard, walking in silence along the path contouring the bay until they see Charlene sitting on the bench near the water. Charlene jumps up, runs over to them and says, "Auntie Anita—" but Auntie Anita holds up her hand again, "Un-unh, not today."

Charlene puts her hand on Anita's. "Yes today. Remember when I was a kid at the juke joint, and we were catching the bottles falling off the table when you were singing "Shake that Shuga," then all of a sudden you started singing about the bay, do you remember? Uncle Gerald, do you remember?"

Auntie Anita and Uncle Gerald tell Charlene they don't know if they remember, and ask Charlene if she's sure she remembers. Charlene is sure. So they ask Charlene to keep walking with them and keep telling them everything. Charlene retells the same memory Auntie Anita and Uncle Gerald had. They make it to Bowfin Street, walk in their house, start up the stairs, and all they hear is Joy, "I'm tellin y'all, a muthafuckin hot sauce bottle just stopped in midair."

Willie Earl says, "Shake that shuga shuga!"

Otis says, "I only remember pops stopped drumming."

Cristal says, "It all makes sense to me because grandma used to say it all the time, there's something in the bay."

Once Auntie Anita, Uncle Gerald, and Charlene reach the top of the stairs, Otis, Joy, Willie Earl, and Cristal stop talking.

Joy breaks the silence, "Auntie, we all had the same memory, except Otis cuz who knows where his mind is, but I hope you remember this . . ."

Uncle Gerald confirms his place in the memory-maybe-real-life, so does Willie Earl, Otis, Joy, and Charlene again. Everyone but Auntie Anita continues to rebuild the memory, yelling over each other, interrupting each other, adding details, subtracting details, correcting each other, saying this didn't happen, but this did, and if that happened then this might mean . . . but what does it really mean, huh, tell me, what does it mean? Auntie Anita tries to listen but is unsettled by all the noise and slips into her and Uncle Gerald's bedroom. She sits at her vanity surrounded by soft bare lightbulbs, and she picks up the rainbow trout brooch made of gemstones off her gold tray that was Betty Lee's, so colorful in her hands, the one she always wore when they performed. She rubs her thumb over the blue gemstone eye of the fish, looks in the mirror, and sees herself and Betty Lee singing at the juke joint [with water at their ankles]

OooOOooOOOOHhhh [the water rises to their waists]

I don't CARE what they SAAAAY [the water completely submerges their bodies]

sumthin's at the bottom of the BAAAAY [bubbles floating out of their mouths as they sing]

The mirror returns to her own reflection. She knows she has to find out what is at the bottom of the bay.

She goes back into the living room where everyone is still yelling, interrupting, and correcting each other. They turn to her and each start firing off questions: What's at the bottom of the bay? What does it mean? Why did you start singing that song?

"I don't know," Auntie Anita says, rubbing her hair back sighing. "I didn't even know I was singing about the bottom of the bay until today."

"Try to remember," Uncle Gerald says.

Joy says, "I wanna know."

"Me too," Willie Earl says.

"I wish y'all woulda asked me in the moment," Auntie Anita says, waving her hand for Joy and Otis to make room for her on the couch. They scoot apart and she sits between them. Willie Earl laughs. "Willie Earl, why you ain't 'HaHa' ya ass over and ask back then? Gerald, why you ain't use that big-ass voice of yours to say 'what was that about, baby?'"

Joy agrees, "I know that's right, Auntie. Willie Earl, you louder than everybody, you sho'nuff shoulda opened your mouth."

"You right, Joy," Willie Earl says. "You surely right."

Uncle Gerald laughs and smacks Willie Earl on the back, "We definitely should have said something then, but now the moment is long gone."

Auntie Anita crosses her legs, "Okay, that's enough, I can't trust my own, or y'all's memory."

Willie Earl says, "So, Anita, you gonna go to the bottom of the nasty-ass bay to see what's there?"

Auntie Anita uncrosses her legs, rests her elbows on her knees and leans forward. "Are YOU gonna go to the bottom of the nasty-ass bay to see what's there, Willie Earl? Goddamn, how about that?"

Willie Earl shakes his head no, while his laugh floats over to the kitchen table where Cora Mae is playing with her cars. She runs her car over the side of the table while singing:

I don't CARE what they SAAAAY
sumthin's at the bottom of the BAAAAY.

July 20

Once upon a time at the top of the Hills, the rich people start lining up at six a.m. Then they start lining up at four a.m. Then they start lining up at two a.m. Then they started lining up at seven p.m. in RVs to camp out to be first in line for the tours, which is all Cristal and Lexus see as they park the bus for the night on top of the ridge.

The rich people from the Hills can't get enough of the tornadoes, can't get enough of the flowers growing teeth, the digital apples, the coffins rattling. Cristal and Lexus begin to notice the slightest changes in the exhibits from day-to-day. The tornado begins to slow down, and peters out before it hits the person furthest away so it blows as cool soft wind. The rainbow bar digital apples keep stalling out and going to static. The twenty-four-karat gold-trimmed trees begin to grow a patina around the trunks. No new exhibits have popped up.

"You would think," Lexus says, "that the novelty of nothing new would wear off on these folks, but look at them." Even though it's dark out, Lexus puts her hand over her eyes like a shield, surveying the rows of RVs waiting to get on the overflow list, those who couldn't reach Willie Earl to get on the day's roster.

"As long as they're coming," Cristal says, grabbing Lexus's hand as they stand on the dirt road around the first switchback of the hills. "I don't care what the reason is. At least they're committed."

The word got out the most thrilling, exciting, interactive art is happening in Tannery Bay with an artist rarely seen in real life, which created the buzz they were hoping for, but this demand is almost too much for everybody. "No new exhibits, because it's clear Auntie Anita is tired."

"Nah, she's not tired," Cristal says. "She's just doing her thing elsewhere, you ate those eggplants from the greenhouse by the juke joint, right? She grew those overnight."

The hill is steep and they slide down slightly, dig their toes into the dirt, grab each other to stabilize. Cristal lets out a little yelp, and a rich lady with the biggest beehive she's ever seen looks down from her window at her and sneers, straightens out her newspaper, takes a drag from her ivory cigarette holder.

They wrap their arms around each other's waists so they each have a hand in each other's back pockets, and keep walking down the hill, around the switchback, to the bottom where Lexus locked up her bike in the alley behind the casino. They see Joy and Merle from Merle's Plumbing, inspecting the pipes coming from the back of the casino into the ground and setting up orange safety cones. Merle is pointing along with whispers and Joy is nodding like she's the best student in class.

Merle and Joy see Lexus and Cristal and nod. They nod back knowingly. Lexus takes the key from around her neck and unchains her bike, and Cristal hops on the seat, grabs Lexus's waist as she stands and pedals toward Bowfin Street.

Cristal squints into the dark up the hillside at the rows of reflective lights on the backs of the bumper-to-bumper RVs and then beyond that to the mansions teetering on the cliff's edge of the Hills as if, at any moment, they will plunge to the bay below, one on top of the other, until there are no more houses, only forest, the bay swallowing and burying lumber and marble, saltwater swimming pools and bad men.

When they get back to the neighborhood, Willie Earl, Otis, and Leviticus are sitting on Willie Earl's balcony. Otis and Leviticus are tinkering with a 35 mm camera, splayed open on the table like it vomited the film. Otis lifts the film with two fingers, then lets it fall sadly while shaking his head and rolling his eyes. Leviticus rubs Otis's neck. "We'll figure it out, let's give it a break."

"How's it lookin up on the hills?" Willie Earl says.

Lexus leans over the balcony. "Ass-to-ass and ball-to-wall."

Willie Earl laughs the laugh that floats over to the hammock in the trees and sways in the July heat. "They just keep comin," he says, "and Anita ain't been through in a hot minute."

Cristal raises her arms. "God! Why does everyone keep acting like Auntie ain't ever okay?" She rolls her eyes at Lexus and Willie Earl and walks off without saying bye, going home. Lexus starts to walk after her but she stops, turns, and walks down the street instead, going to see Whatshername. Otis rolls his eyes at both of them, but thinks, they need to quit pussyfooting around, then he looks at Leviticus's smile and thinks again, shit, who am I to talk, I was pussyfooting around with Leviticus forever.

"Heyyy Leviticus," Otis says standing. "I'll be back, Imma go talk to Cristal for a minute, then hopefully we can get the camera to work. I love you, thank you for being you."

Willie Earl says, "Tell Cristal I'm sorry, she's right, Anita is fine." He runs his hand over his stubbly face, takes a cigar out of the pocket of his overalls and taps it on the table while Otis goes across the street. He says "I'm sho'll glad you and Otis got each other. I know a thang or two about love, I tell you what."

"I appreciate you, Willie Earl, and I'm glad we got each other, too. But he's still all tangled about this foolish plan as he calls it, he don't think it's gonna work," Leviticus says.

"Hell, I don't blame him. It's hard to keep up with Joy's brain, girl is sharp, but you gotta be even sharper to follow. I'm with Otis though, cuz I'm little worried too cuz we ain't seen Anita. But with no new exhibits, they still comin, so I guess we got that going for us." He lights his cigar, and his laugh floats back from the hammock and settles into the potted soil and his peppers start to glow, and grow a half an inch. "It's only a matter of time before them Owners come sniffin around because we ain't took nobody to see the art at their casino."

Across the street, Otis knocks on his old bedroom/Cristal's current bedroom door. She stuffs her face into a pillow when he opens the door and she sees it's him. "I know you don't like me, Otis, because I stole your room and your family or whatever, so you didn't have to come over here and rub it in, I know, I know."

"The gag is I do, actually, like you. I mean, you irk me bad!" Otis says, still standing in the doorway. "Look, baby, I'm sorry, I've been terrible to you."

"For real?"

"For real," he says running his hand along his old doorframe, still loving the sturdiness. "I've been judging how you and Lexus always be, and it was wrong of me. You never shut up about her! It ain't fair, though, to always be mad at you about it. Y'alls time will come, like me and Levi. I got all tied up on her player ways. I don't want to see you get hurt."

"Thank you. I don't know what's up with Lexus."

"Me either, but if you need me to shake some sense into her, let me know, or let Joy know cuz I ain't good at shaking sense into anything. Don't talk about her no more!"

Cristal laughs. "I hear you. I definitely will let you know."

"Alright, Imma get back over there and try to get this camera working. You're gonna get through, I promise. It'll all work out, or not," Otis winks at her and shuts the door.

Meanwhile, far up in the tippy-top of the hills, in Lime-Green Velour Robe's house, Reflecting Mirror mindlessly scratches his crotch as if no one can see him even though his colleagues can and are watching with disgust. He is thinking about those young girls he saw holding hands in their short, short jean shorts earlier walking along the RVs. He's leering in his mind, which reads on his face, which he tightens up after he realizes his colleagues are watching him. "Can you not?" one of them says.

They are sitting around a boardroom overlooking the swimming pool. Bald Spot 'n' Goatee reaches for the pen in his shirt pocket and realizes the pen has leaked and his shirt is stained blue, which he tries to cover by pulling his suit coat tighter but can't quite make it shut, so it continues to flap open showing the blue expanding by the second, and what he doesn't realize is he has the bottom of the pen in his mouth so ink is on his chin, on the corners of his mouth, middle of his lips.

Golden Chalice is helping himself to coffee across the room, spilling it mostly on the boardroom table but getting some in his golden chalice. He farts loudly.

Meanwhile, Lime-Green Velour Robe is slightly sweaty, swaying left to right then right to left in his executive chair, impatiently.

Delores the housekeeper enters to refresh the beverages and cookies. Lime-Green Velour Robe tries to trip her, but she catches the water and coffee from flying onto the floor. She cusses them out under her breath, remembering her new mission to listen closely and gather information. She leaves the room, but only momentarily.

Meanwhile, Birthmark with the Gun is cleaning the gun and loading it with bullets. Occasionally he points it at the head of Bald Spot 'n' Goatee when he thinks no one is looking.

Shiny Shoes, Reflection Mirror, and XXX take their seats at either end of the table. "Are all of the Owners here?" Lime-Green Velour Robe says. They all mumble in various degrees of agreement. "Townsend Tourstiques is growing faster than anyone could have imagined! We hear the rumor mill here in the Hills! Every Tom, Dick, and Harry at the country club is raving! And it is hurting our business at the casino. There are whispers the tannery is going to suffer if the tours get any larger!" he says.

Golden Chalice says, "So, what do you propose we do?"

When Delores returns with a new tray of snacks and drinks, Lime-Green Velour Robe says, "We must approach Townsend with a new offer for the Artist. We must make him an offer they cannot refuse."

Bald Spot 'n' Goatee says, "What if they refuse?"

Delores goes to the big table, pouring coffee and water, listening.

Birthmark with the Gun points the gun at Bald Spot 'n' Goatee and says, "We don't let them," and then they each laugh.

After the meeting, after the last colleague has left, Lime-Green Velour Robe finds a cockle shell outside of his door. He picks it up in disgust and throws it down the driveway. Later, when he gets into bed, another one appears on his bedside table. "What the . . ." he says and takes the cockle shell into the bathroom, drops it into the toilet, flushes it, and puts the lid down. Standing at the marble urinal next to the toilet, he pees while thinking about Townsend and how he's going to get him. Pee splashes back on him, lightly at first and then heavily, and when he looks down cockle shells geyser from the urinal drain, uppercutting him and knocking him to the floor. The shells keep pinging the ceiling and plummeting on him while he tries to get up, but he keeps slipping and falling in his pee and cockle shells.

July 21

Once upon a time in the dilapidated casino, Otis is dealing blackjack, and Leviticus is at the table next to him dealing three-card poker, their last few hands of the night, nervous about the next phase of Joy and Uncle Gerald's plan. They know the water is about to come.

Since Otis and Leviticus finally got on the same shift a couple of weeks ago, they've been cheating to let the customers win more as Joy had instructed. In order to keep the suspicion off of only Otis and Leviticus at the card tables, Joy paid the maintenance women to tinker with the slots to allow the customers to win more, then lose more, but ultimately to win more.

Before Lexus quit as casino maintenance to work for the bus tour, she, Joy, and Charlene would go down into the sewer to clog up the casino and tannery pipes. In the middle of the night, they would slide into their waders and slip into the manhole between the tannery and the police station. Uncle Gerald and Rashaad would pass down bags of clay and sand from Rashaad's tow truck. Merle placed wheelbarrows and trowels in the sewage during her "routine maintenance checks." Lexus, Joy, and Charlene wheelbarrowed the clay and sand up the sewer, sloshing to the tannery first, troweling layers and layers of clay/sand into the mouth of the pipes. Then they'd wheelbarrow up further to the casino and do the same. Then climb out of the manhole by the bridge.

In the morning, Merle would get calls from the managers of the tannery and the casino to come figure out the problem. Merle said, "Who knows how old these pipes are! It's possible, no quite possible, no it's guaranteed there's some heavy calcification due the limestone in the water and other solidified ions commonly found in urine, and I'm sure some of those people got some bricks coming out of their bottoms if you know what I mean, which I'm sure you do . . ."

The managers said, "Fix it at once!"

Merle said, "I'll be there ASAP! Yes, it's unquestionable, quite certain, certainly possible it's been a problem all over the bay." Then Merle would go up into the Hills, making sure her truck was visible to the Owners, and pretend to work on the sewage for a few hours, then she'd head down to the tannery and clink around for a bit, then off to the casino for another assessment. The next day, Lexus, Joy, and Charlene would meet Merle in the sewer to remove the clay, until the next time they did it, making the casino and the tannery shut down for two days each time, losing money. Losing money because they aren't in operation, but also because they had to pay Merle's Plumbing: Getting Your Shit Together, Est. July.

Otis nods at Leviticus, Leviticus nods back. Otis feels the keys on the key ring in his pocket—nonfunctional replicas the same weight and number of keys as the key ring the Floor Manager carries clipped to his right belt loop. Leviticus reaches under his table and grabs a small black canvas bag containing thin black gloves and a 35 mm camera wrapped in a plastic bag. They start to walk toward the hall leading to the Floor Manager's office. Otis stands on one side, Leviticus stands on the other and sets the bag on a table.

Charlene is at Merle's office waiting by the phone.

Joy is waiting in the alley behind the casino.

Merle is in the bottom of the casino waiting at the pipes for the sewage backflow preventer. She's been there all night. Otis snuck her in, and stashed two black umbrellas in the janitors closet during shift change, while Leviticus told the floor managers and the security guards to come outside and break up a fake gang fight between Queers on Gears and, well, other members of Queers on Gears who called themselves Baddie Daddies.

"There's a new gang in town!" they kept yelling. "The Baddie Daddies are in this bitch!"

The Queers on Gears yelled back, "This is our territory!" and they threw glass bottles near each other but not at each other.

Floor Manager Number One yelled, "This is nobody's territory! This is the private property of Tannery Bay Casino!"

Both gangs threw bottles at him. One bottle hit him in the head and one hit him in the shoulder. The other hit him in the shin. He ducked and ran, limped off. Leviticus bypassed him, grabbed him by his shirt collar and said, "Do something! They're endangering us all! They are terrorizing our patrons!" Floor Manager Number One scrambled away falling once, twice, three times before finally getting his feet underneath him. He ran to the parking lot, got into his car, and drove off.

Merle can hear the water pressing against the metal flap of the backflow preventer inside the large pipe. She loosens the screws on the outside of the pipe so the flap opens. Water rushes through, up to all the bathrooms, to the toilets, and geysers to the ceiling. Water geysers out of the sinks in the bathrooms, out of the sinks at the bars. The pressure pops the sprinkler heads off and it downpours while a wave of water rushes onto the main casino floor. People start screaming and flailing and stealing chips. The security guards start telling everyone to evacuate. Floor Manager Number Two runs out of the office, making sure to lock the door, then clips the key ring back on his right belt loop. He runs down the hall, about to enter the main floor, but Leviticus sticks his foot out and trips him. Floor Manager Number Two falls face down into the brown water. "Are you okay, sir!" Otis says. Leviticus acts like he is trying to help him up but keeps pushing his head down, water splashing in his mouth and eyes. He pushes his head down again. Otis pulls the key ring out of his pocket, unclips Floor Manager Number Two's key ring, then replaces it with the fake key ring. He pushes his head down a third time. They finally pull him to his feet. "We gotta get you outta here," Leviticus yells, and shoves him toward the door. Floor Manager Number Two runs out coughing. Leviticus grabs the black bag from the table, and he and Otis run down the hall toward the office, stopping to unlock the janitor's closet for umbrellas.

Otis glances around to make sure no one is watching, but Merle has just come out of the basement and is standing in the doorway at the end of the hall. They nod at each other. Otis unlocks the door and he and Leviticus go in, and find the waist-high steel cabinet in the corner. Umbrellas open. Unlock the cabinet. And there it is sitting on a sliding tray: the burgundy leather ledger book.

Otis holds both umbrellas over Leviticus while he puts on the black gloves, unwraps the camera, slides out the tray, and flips to the back of the book. Snaps pictures of the earnings and losses. There's a lot of red. Leviticus keeps snapping pictures of each page going back ten Julys. He closes the book, slides the tray back, wraps the camera back in the plastic bag. Gloves off. Otis locks the cabinet. Umbrellas closed. Crack open the door and peek out. Only Merle. They run out and lock the door, pass off the bag, umbrellas, and key ring to Merle.

Otis and Leviticus run back down the hall and out of the front to join the other evacuees. Merle runs out of the back and into the alley, passes the key ring to Joy, then disappears with the bag to the opposite end of the alley toward the bridge headed to Bowfin Street. Joy circles around the building to the crowd and finds Otis and Leviticus standing next to Floor Manager Number Two who is still coughing and rubbing his eyes. Joy bumps Floor Manager Number Two while Otis unclips the fake key ring and Joy replaces it with the real key ring. They push out of the back of the crowd and head toward Bowfin Street.

At Merle's office, the phone rings and Charlene answers flatly, "Merle's Plumbing: Getting Your—"

"This is an emergency!"

"Sir, I need to finis—"

"It's an emerg—"

"I hate to be interrupted," Charlene says. "If you interrupt me one more time I will hang up on you! Now where was I? Yes, this is Merle's Plumbing: Getting Your Shit Together since July, how may I assist you? Would you like to try our VIP bundle service package?"

"Come quickly! The casino is flooded."

"Interesting, so is the tannery, and some residential areas in the Hills—it's a problem all over the bay, friend. We will get to you in the order your call was received. Have a blessed day and thank you for choosing Merle's Plumbing: Getting Your Shit Together."

Back on Bowfin Street at Auntie Anita and Uncle Gerald's, the whole crew is there. Merle has finally stopped panting, Otis and Leviticus are soaked, and Joy is looking at the camera sitting in the middle of the table next to a bowl of eggplants and potatoes and leeks from Anita's installation. Uncle Gerald says he's gonna go get the photos developed. Leviticus says, "There's a lot of information there, on the casino, the tannery, even the newspaper."

Otis says, "Damn near everything is in red, nothing has been making money."

Uncle Gerald says, "How do you suspect they gonna buy the bus tour if they don't have money?"

July 22

Once upon a time up in the Hills above the broke-ass flooded casino, the morning pink sun illuminates Lime-Green Velour Robe as he sits alone at the board table, tapping his fingers on the burgundy leather ledger book, waiting for the other men to show up.

Delores has walked all the way up the Hills, past the long line of people waiting for Townsend Touristiques, and she enters the house. The wife of Lime-Green Velour Robe gave her specific instructions to arrive early to set up gin, whiskey, and vodka in the middle of the table. Today she has requested Delores remain in the room the entire time. Fine by me, Delores thinks, I can get more information from these clowns.

The Owners start to arrive, and Delores feeds them booze. Lime-Green Velour Robe stares straight ahead as they get settled, still tapping the ledger. Birthmark with the Gun starts to speak, but Lime-Green Velour Robe interrupts him.

"Did I tell you to fucking talk?" Lime-Green Velour Robe says. The whole room comes to a halt. Even Delores, who takes a seat immediately.

"No," Birthmark with the Gun says.

"Then why are you still talking!" Lime-Green Velour Robe says.

He shuts up and sinks back into his chair. "Gin!" he says, even though his tumbler is half-full. Delores balls and unballs her fist, takes a deep breath, gets gin from the center of the table, and fills his glass. She thinks, I hope you fuckin choke you ol lowlife, greedy, gooseneck peckerwood. I oughta knock your head clean off and punt the muthafucka over the hill.

The man gulps the gin until it's gone. It's oozing out his mouth and down his robe. He wiggles the glass in the air indicating more. Delores refills the glass. He slams the glass down, spilling everywhere. He opens the ledger book and turns it to face the other men. "We're done. Finito!" He throws the book at XXX and Shiny Shoes's heads, they duck, and the book slams into the window.

He goes on, "There are no profits from the casino, the tannery, and the newspaper. Nothing. We've been bleeding out money for maintenance. The casino and tannery are down indefinitely. It will take forever to get those operational, and even longer to turn a new profit. The only thing making money in this town is the art tour and goddamn jerkoff Townsend. Where," he slams his fist on the table, making everyone wince, "is!" slam "the!" slam "profit!"

Golden Chalice says, "So, what do you propose—"

"What do *I* propose? More like what do *you* propose. Exactly why I brought you imbeciles here. Get to proposing!"

Everyone drinks instead of thinking, requesting more from Delores. After several fast rounds, no one says anything. They all look obliterated.

"I said propose!"

Reflection Mirror says "Umm . . . umm . . ."

"I said propose!"

Bald Spot 'n' Goatee says, "Well, actually, if we . . . umm . . ."

"I said propose!"

XXX says, "Just to play devil's advocate here, what if . . . umm . . ."

"I said propose!"

Birthmark with the Gun says, "Kill Townsend. It's simple really."

Delores catches her eyes as they go wide. Relax your face babe, she thinks, keep it cool, don't let on, act like you didn't hear nothin. She gets up to try to leave.

"Sit down," Lime-Green Velour Robe says. She sits back down.

"Simple?" Lime-Green Velour Robe says, "Well, why don't you elaborate on this simple idea you have."

Birthmark puts his gun on the table, facing the barrel across at Golden Chalice and Reflecting Mirror, who inch out of the way. Birthmark slides the gun to keep the aim on the men. "We find the Artist at night, follow her at a distance, and she'll lead us to Townsend. We kill him, put him where no one will find him, dissolve him in the chemical vats at the tannery, then pour him into the bay with the rest. Once Townsend is gone, you, sir, can swoop in and 'save' the art tour."

"I like where your head is . . ." Lime-Green Velour Robe rolls the idea around for a few seconds. "Good. We never see Townsend and the Artist without each other, so of course she will lead us to him. I wouldn't be surprised if the uppity sonuvabitch didn't sit on the floor next to her feet while she takes a shit!" He scratches his head and downs another glass of gin and Delores comes over to refill it. He continues. "We, I mean *you*, need to kill Townsend alone, and not hurt the Artist. We need her."

"I don't think Townsend is with her at night because—" says Birthmark with the Gun.

"Find out! I don't want you to think. Find her tonight! If you don't, look for her the next night, and the next, and the next, until you do!"

All the Owners say, "Well done! Huzzah! Excellent plan, sir! Genius!"

"Don't 'excellent plan' me," Lime-Green Velour Robe says. "We need to find out all we can, so each of you will station yourselves at the existing exhibits to observe how it all works. Perhaps you will catch the Artist doing maintenance. Record if she acts alone, and if not, is Townsend helping, or the workers? Don't hurt the workers. We need them, and soon they will need us."

Delores gets up and slowly makes her way out of the room, this time with no one stopping her. She gathers her things, creeps down the hallway, almost to the front door, when the wife of Lime-Green Velour Robe stops her.

"Silly goose, the meetings aren't over. They will be there all day, and probably well into the night. Now hustle on back in there!" She grabs Delores by the shoulders and turns her around.

Delores takes a step, and over her shoulder says, "Would you mind if I make a phone call real quick to check on my son? I would be so grateful. He was sick earlier and I want to make sure his illness has not progressed." The wife's face drops. She is not pleased. She grimaces and says, "Be fast."

Delores walks down the hall to the kitchen, and the woman follows tightly behind, entering to open cupboards pretending to have a reason to be there with her. She lifts the phone from the receiver, sticks her finger in hole number five, and turns the dialer clockwise. When she's about to dial the next number, she looks over her shoulder and sees the wife standing next to the sink, mouthing, "I hope everything is okay." Delores finishes dialing, turns her back to her, and the phone rings three times before Uncle Gerald picks up.

"Gerald and Anita's residence, state yo business."

Delores says, "Hey there sis, it's me, calling from the Hills, is my precious baby feeling alright? I am worried about him so."

"Delores, that you?"

"I am only making sure his illness has not taken a turn for the worse. I would hate for my little darling to fall so ill."

"What the hell are you talking about?"

"Oh, wonderful! Simply marvelous! Thank you! Tell him I love him and Mommy will be home soon!

"Del—"

Delores hangs up the phone, turns to the woman and says, "He's feeling much better."

"Such fantastic news," the wife says. "Such a shame. It must be so hard to be a working mother, spending so much time away from your little ones. I wouldn't know! Stuck inside this house all the time and all! Skip on back to the boardroom, I know they are dying without their specially made drinks!" The woman hands Delores a plate of cookies freshly baked by the other housekeeper early this morning.

Delores walks back down the hall, I gotta get out of here she thinks. As soon as she opens the door to the boardroom, she hears Lime-Green Velour Robe yelling, "Splendid! That will be the second part of the plan." Damn, Delores thinks, I missed something.

Down from the Hills, across the bridge, Otis and Leviticus sit on the bench overlooking the bay.

They're holding hands in the exact position that the lady in waders showed him, and Otis rubs Leviticus's small scars on his index finger. Otis puts his head on Leviticus's shoulder and Leviticus kisses the top of Otis's head. Otis keeps an eye on Cora Mae throwing rocks. Each time she throws a rock, it lands on the surface with a thud, stays there for a second, then slowly sinks into the gel water. She asks Otis to get more rocks for her, and Otis and Leviticus both get up and fill the bottom of their shirts with rocks so Cora Mae can have enough.

They resume their positions on the bench, and Cora Mae keeps throwing. Uncle Gerald comes walking up behind them,

"Hey! I got a call from Delores talking about her nonexistent son? Something is wrong, it's like she was trying to tell me something but couldn't say. Where Joy at?"

Otis says, "She's in the sewer doing who knows what."

Uncle Gerald sits next to Leviticus. "We gotta get somebody up on that hill to make sure Delores is alright. Y'all go find Merle, ask her to go up there on a 'routine maintenance check' and tell her to see if she can find Delores."

Otis says, "Cora Mae, let's go, baby . . . Cora Mae . . . Cora Mae!"

Cora Mae can't hear them. She's transfixed by the water. She only hears the water whispering her name, Cora Mae, Cora Mae. "Cora Mae!" Uncle Gerald yells. "When you get so hardheaded, baby?" Cora Mae still doesn't hear him. She drops her rocks.

"I guess she gotta get her last throw in," Leviticus says.

Cora Mae keeps walking, step, step, until one foot touches the water. Uncle Gerald, Otis, and Leviticus shoot up off the bench and start running to her, yelling her name. By the time they reach her, she's in up to her knees. They yank her back out. She looks down at her wet pants and starts to cry.

Gerald says, "I'll take her to Joy. Y'all go find Merle."

Otis and Leviticus go up the path, cross the bridge, and see Merle's truck in front of the casino. They look around to make sure no one is watching, then duck under the yellow caution tape crisscrossing the faux gold archway. The flood line is almost to the ceiling, slot machines are knocked over, the poker and blackjack tables are waterlogged, and the floors are slicked with brown. There are lines of footprints going back and forth from the door to the hall where the Floor Manager's office is. They follow from the main floor, down the hall, past the Floor Manager's office, and to the door leading to the basement. Creak it open, and walk down. They see Merle turning a socket wrench on the backflow preventer. "Merle," Otis says. She turns around, "Oh, it's y'all! I heard the door and thought it was somebody from the casino so I was pretending to work hard. Whew!" They tell her what's going on with Delores and what Uncle Gerald wants her to do, and she says, "I'm on it!" and runs out to her truck.

Merle gets to the top of the hill and drives in front of the house. Delores sees her truck out of the big window, please stop, Merle, please stop, she thinks. Delores loses sight of her truck. The Owners are arguing over when the murder should happen in the first or second part of the plan. Delores can hardly hear the doorbell over the shouting and banging on the table. She gets up, goes to the door, and opens it. Merle.

Merle says, "I heard, no I was told, no I know there are issues with the plumbing up here I need to fix."

Before Delores can answer, the wife steps in front of her.

"Good morning!" the wife says. "Can I help you with anything?"

"Good morning to you ma'am, we are out here doing some routine maintenance checks to check on that which needs to be checked on to root out the root of the source of the source of the problem all of Tannery Bay is having today you see," Merle says.

"I think we're all okay here," the wife says. She looks at Delores suspiciously. Delores smiles.

"Are you sure? Very sure? Extremely sure?" Merle says. "Everything is right as rain? Peaches? Clear skies all around?"

Delores nods yes.

The wife says, "My husband is in the middle of an extremely private and important meeting. He has requested no interruptions."

"Terrific, outstanding," Merle says looking at Delores. "Outstanding?"

"Outstanding," Delores says.

"Now run on back, goose," the wife says to Delores without looking at her, leaning against the door, watching Merle walk back to her truck. "I'll take care of it from here."

Delores goes back into the boardroom. Merle leaves to go tell Uncle Gerald that Delores is safe, she probably had something to say about the meeting but wasn't able to leave, but the important thing is she's safe, and she'll probably be home soon to tell us whatever she needs to.

Delores is still in the boardroom refilling and refilling drinks and listening and listening to the men argue and argue and come up with no new solid plans for hours and hours until the pink sun sets.

"I'm done with you morons for the night," Lime-Green Velour Robe says, "get out of here." He stops Birthmark with the Gun, leans close to him, and says, "You know what to do, and I want you to start immediately."

All the Owners leave. The wife comes in and tells Delores she is free to go.

Delores walks out of the house, wanting to run, but doesn't want them to notice her, so she keeps walking until she's out of view of the house, then takes off running down the hill, taking switchback after switchback until she's at the bottom by the casino.

She looks for Merle's truck, hoping she can get a ride across the bridge. No truck. She runs over to the tannery. No truck. She runs back up the street to the casino, across the bridge, takes the shortcut through the graveyard, and out onto Bowfin Street. Without knocking, she busts into Uncle Gerald and Auntie Anita's house, runs up the stairs, and finds Uncle Gerald, Otis, Joy, Willie Earl, and Cora Mae at the dining room table.

Delores is panting. "They wanna kill you, Willie Earl," she says, bending over with her hands on her knees. "They wanna follow the Artist and kill Townsend. Why I was calling."

Joy says, "The Artist don't exist, so they can't follow you."

"Auntie Anita is real," Delores says, "and if they catch her they'll know she's the real artist."

"Where's Anita?" Delores says. "We gotta tell her to stop."

"She already left for the night," Uncle Gerald says.

"We gotta go find her," Joy says. "Delores and Willie Earl, y'all can't be seen with us, so stay here with Cora Mae. C'mon Otis and Leviticus, and you, too, Uncle Gerald." Uncle Gerald was already putting on his shoes before Joy said his name.

Back across the bridge, in the middle of the street at the bottom of the hill, Auntie Anita is standing with a paint roller at the end of a long stick, rolling red onto the pavement. Birthmark with the Gun is walking down the hill when he hears the paint roller moving back and forth. He peers over the hill but can only make out a shadowy figure. He turns another switchback, but figures it'd take too long on the road, so he steps over the edge into the dirt in order to get down faster. He steps without sound until the heel of his right foot slips noisy on the gravel and he falls backward. Auntie Anita hears the slip, drops the paint roller, and takes off running toward the alley shadows behind the casino. Birthmark with the Gun keeps running straight down through the dirt until he falls again and tumbles out into the street where Auntie Anita was. He stands and sees a picture of a half-painted cockle shell. He bends over, dips his pinky into the wet red paint, brings it to his nose to sniff, then licks the paint while looking around with his eyes narrowed.

July 23

Once upon a time across the bridge past the graveyard and the molded and mildewing casino, past the tannery with its churning purple vats, up into the hills at the edge of the forest a trail of cockle shells leads the morning tour into the clearing with the rows of folding chairs.

Couples split off, women hang on their husbands' arms and smile. No one sees the cockle shells except for Lexus and Cristal, who pick them up when no one is looking. "Keep moving along, folks, the exhibit is about to begin," Lexus says.

The trees above her rustle. On a branch the woman in waders cascades cockle shells down like snowflakes. The shells land in the women's hair, slip down the collars of the men's shirts, but no one notices the heft or ting. The woman with the waders flashes her eyes with a moving picture of a baby walking on water. The baby looks familiar, Cristal thinks, but quickly moves ahead of the women, picks the shells from their hair as gently as she can, guides them to their seats.

Lexus starts the spiel of don't touch anything, keep hands and feet inside your seat, relax and enjoy. Neither of them notices, at first, the two men in the far back corner because all the men who take the tour look exactly the same. A sneer in one of their eyes, even through heavy black sunglasses, strikes Lexus as odd. A man with shiny shoes and greasy hair with the strangest smirk on his face. When they are walking down the aisles, Lexus grabs Cristal's hand and doesn't let go until they are on the bus.

She keeps watching out the back windows, and the man keeps looking behind him, moving his neck almost unnaturally, each look backward his neck going a little farther than it is supposed to. She doesn't say anything to Cristal, but keeps her close, holding her around the waist, keeping her on her lap when she tries to get up.

Shiny Shoes rams his elbow into XXX next to him. He elbows him two, three times without saying anything. "The hell!" XXX says. Even though those two young girls told them to put their belongings away, he has his porn magazine out reading it like a newspaper. Shiny Shoes slaps the magazine out of his hands.

Everyone is getting restless. A man on the other side of the aisle yells "Come on, we're waiting!" Someone else boos. "The girls?" Shiny Shoes asks. "Do you think either of them could be the Artist? Should we kidnap one of them?"

"No dumbass, we already know what the Artist looks like. Besides, the Artist would never be here in stark daylight, preposterous."

Shiny Shoes elbows XXX again, but this time hard right into the ribs. XXX coughs. "We should kidnap them as ransom," says Shiny Shoes. "If you want this gangly green-haired girl back, we'll tell them, give us the Artist."

XXX wheezes a laugh through his labored breath at getting elbowed so hard. "But don't we want Townsend?" XXX says, and Shiny Shoes elbows him again. "Stop with the hitting, I got it," and he doubles over himself, drool dangling from his mouth as he aspirates.

"We are going to take the green-haired girl as soon as this thing is done," Shiny Shoes says. "No, we are going to take her right now," he says, as he fights to take the seatbelt off, pulling and banging the seat up and down to get out.

In front of them, behind them, to the sides of them, the tornado begins rumbling. "Finally!" the man across the aisle says and his wife gives a small woop in celebration. The sky turns pink to green with streaks of gray. The wind whips fast and hard, eliminating all sound, including when Shiny Shoes starts yelling at XXX about how they need to go now and kidnap the green-haired girl.

A woman in the front forgot to take off her dangling earrings which get torn out of her ears but no one can hear her screaming in pain. The wind barrels down the trees, crack and crash. The ground rumbles, chairs shake. Someone topples over. The rain starts at the outer edges of the forest. They can hear it before they can see it. The wind stops immediately. The rain is visible and then it is not. Silence. Right as they can all faintly hear the woman crying over her bleeding ears and Shiny Shoes saying "We have to get out of here!" the tornado funnel clouds rumble from three directions, moving from the sky to the ground like toy tops, lurching a bit before they even themselves out, get on course. The tornadoes rip the ground in its well-worn paths, moving fast, just like Auntie Anita has designed them to do.

Shiny Shoes lifts the seat, the chair fastened to his body by the seatbelt. He walks into the aisle, using all of his strength to try to break the polyester fabric apart. He's thrashing the back of the chair on the ground to break the legs, which will not budge. No one can see him but Lexus and Cristal, safe in the bus, because everyone has their heads down to avoid getting hit in the face and eyes. XXX has stopped fighting. Shiny Shoes charges his body backward, right into the middle of the tornado. The tornadoes follow their path and evaporate.

Once the sky is back to pink, Lexus and Cristal hop out of the back of the bus. The fun of the tornado exhibit is everyone is so shocked and discombobulated afterward most of the time no one has anything to say and usually comply with what they order them to do next with no complaints. They direct them that it is safe to unlatch their seatbelts and go to the next exhibit. XXX slyly looks around for his friend as to not draw attention to himself. There is the green-haired girl, so clearly he didn't abduct her. He steps on his magazine, breaking the pages apart under his feet. When he looks up to the top of the tree line, there dangles Shiny Shoes, his neck hanging and angled in a way that no neck should hang and angle, splayed out along the canopy of lush green leaves. XXX glances quickly but keeps moving in line.

Behind them, a trail of cockle shells follows into the bus.

Later that evening, XXX leaves a goodbye letter to Lime-Green Velour Robe in his mailbox. He jumps off the bay bridge. No one notices.

July 24

Once upon a time across the bridge from the molded and mildewing casino, on Bowfin Street, Uncle Gerald walks into his house whistling, carrying under his arm a thick manila folder stuffed inside of the *Tannery Bay Daily*.

Delores, not Artist Delores or Housekeeper Delores, just regular ol Delores, walks into Uncle Gerald and Auntie Anita's a few minutes later carrying a bag with her housekeeper uniform. She'd just gotten off work up in the Hills.

Everyone else is already there except Merle who's still walking back and forth between the casino and the tannery pretending to work. Whenever one of the men involved with the casino asks about progress, she rambles off a bunch of technical language about water pressure, variable frequency drives, vacuum breakers, and how the backflow valves are reversing the ionization polarity causing irreparable corrosive damage to the copper converters. The men agree with whatever she says by repeating the terms back to her and nodding seriously because they don't want to seem stupid. Merle chuckles to herself because a copper converter doesn't even exist, which makes her remember the day Golden Chalice patted an iron pipe and said, "Indeed, this copper converter sure is damaged beyond repair."

When Delores was at work, she heard Golden Chalice report to Lime-Green Velour Robe that the copper valves caused damage to the vacuum-ionized backflow system, and it is beyond repair frequency due to corrosive damage, which made her laugh knowing none of it was real.

Lime-Green Velour Robe said, "I've heard. Those vacuum-ionized backflows are serious problems."

Golden Chalice said, "Indeed they are, sir. Indeed they are."

Cora Mae is at the table with a purple crayon drawing a picture of the bay. Auntie Anita is the only one watching her draw the squiggly water lines with fish underneath with triangle tails. As soon as she starts drawing a stick figure at the bottom of the water, Uncle Gerald takes the manila folder from the newspaper and spreads the contents on the table: the developed photos of the ledger book Otis and Leviticus snapped. The photos are black and white, which means they can't see the red ink, but all the negative signs confirm what Otis and Leviticus saw and what Housekeeper Delores heard: the casino and tannery are in the red. The old fishery has a constant zero, not even a value of what the building itself is worth. Cora Mae has stopped drawing.

Joy arranges the photos in descending order, going back from July to July for ten Julys, noticing the spending patterns, the floor winnings/losses, the constant spending on tanning hides no one buys, and the recent, consistent dumps of money to Merle's Plumbing.

"This ain't good," Joy says to no one in particular, running her finger up and down the columns. "There's no money to buy the bus tour. Our plan is gonna fall apart."

"They still want the bus tour!" Delores says. "They just wanna kill for it, not buy it, that's what I told y'all already."

Uncle Gerald asks, "Did you hear any more about the part of the plan you missed, Delores?"

"They haven't mentioned it again," she says.

Otis waves his arms like calling a time out, "Let's shut this whole operation down. I told y'all the plan was foolish."

"No!" says Joy shuffling the pictures. "We've done too much already to quit."

Willie Earl says, "You gotta know when to stop, cuz I sho'nuff don't wanna get killed."

"I know that's right," Auntie Anita says. "We gonna shut it all down tomorrow. Cristal and Lexus, don't y'all get on the bus in the morning."

Joy circles three areas of income throughout the months: "Look at this . . ."

Everyone leans in closer, except Cora Mae. Joy goes on, "Right here, where did this big-ass amount of money come from?"

While everyone is talking, Cora Mae takes her bay drawing off the table and walks down the stairs. "Now if you go back to this Addendum page, it says, Real Estate Sum and Rentals," Joy says.

Cora Mae leaves the house, starts walking down the street.

"They've been selling their houses, and I think using rental income to keep the business afloat!"

Cora Mae keeps walking.

"So if they're willing to give up property for they funky-ass businesses, then they'd definitely do the same for our business!"

Auntie Anita can't get her mind off Cora Mae's drawing, so she looks down to see it, but doesn't find it, looks to the couch, "Where's Cora Mae!" and she looks in the bedroom, the bathroom.

Everybody starts yelling "Cora Mae!" and rushes outside once they realize Cora Mae isn't in the house. Once they are all outside, running down the street toward the bay, they keep calling for her, but Cora Mae can't hear them. She keeps walking. They catch up to her when she's a few feet away from the woman in waders. Joy snatches Cora Mae back from the water, "I had just about enough of you!

This is my baby!" she says. They all see the woman flash her eyes with a moving picture of a baby walking on water. Cora Mae holds the drawing out to the woman, and the woman floats forward to take it but Joy snatches Cora Mae off the ground, puts her on her hip, and starts back to the house with everyone trailing behind her except Auntie Anita. Auntie Anita inches closer to get a better look at the images flashing in the woman's eyes, but far away Cora Mae yells over Joy's shoulder, "Auntie!" and stretches both arms out to her. When Auntie Anita looks back to the water, the woman has vanished.

July 25

Once upon a time behind the broke-ass casino, Lexus walks toward the forest. She holds her nose with her fuchsia bandana because even though the casino and tannery are not running, the air smells like mildew. When she reaches the forest behind the casino, she walks down a one-way dirt road until the forest moves itself out of the way to create a clearing for the magnolia exhibit. Lexus walks up to the nearest oak tree and thanks it, giving some love. She doesn't want to hug it, she ain't no tree-hugging hippie, but she does want to say thank you, she believes in gratitude. Thank you trees, she says aloud, thank you forest, thank you ground, thank you sky and clouds and you, too, you stupid, hot sun. The tops of the trees shake in response. She stuffs the bandana into her back left pocket.

Lexus pulls her harmonica from her back pocket and sits in the middle of the clearing playing "Oh, My Darling Clementine" while she waits for Cristal and the bus to arrive. Willie Earl's laugh rustles from the treetops, sings along in harmonies with her. She is done setting up the chairs for the exhibit. She lays on her back and thinks about Cristal, sticks the end of the harmonica in her mouth and drums her chest. Her hand hits something hard in the front pocket of her overalls, and she pulls it out—a note from Cristal which Lexus had forgotten about. She puts the note on her forehead and closes her eyes. Cristal had slipped her this note last week, but she wanted to act nonchalant so she put it in her front pocket and then told her she was meeting up with Whatsername, when she wasn't actually meeting up with her, she just wanted to play games to make Cristal jealous. Why am I playing games? she thinks, when I could buy her some flowers and tell her how I feel?

All around Lexus sprout sunflowers, moving their heads toward her as if listening. Willie Earl's laugh dances in the sunflowers, making the yellow heads grow. They breathe in and breathe out with her breath. A single, shriveled, yellow petal falls onto the top of her hand. She swats at it. When she opens her eyes, the sunflowers are gone and she can hear the bus coughing up the hill.

The bus ambles to a stop and Reflecting Mirror adjusts his tanning mirror under his chin. Sitting next to him is Bald Spot 'n' Goatee who offers sunscreen to Reflecting Mirror who refuses. They heard at the country club Townsend would be making an appearance on the tour today. They are going to kill him on the spot, Reflecting Mirror thinks, I don't know how since we don't have any weapons on us, dumbass here didn't bring a gun. Bald Spot 'n' Goatee thinks I don't know how we are going to kill Townsend, fuckface here didn't bring a gun. They look at each other and smile big, toothy smiles, a gold tooth flashing in Reflecting Mirror's mouth.

Cristal parks the bus, lays the rules down. There are only return customers on the bus today, except two men Lexus has never seen on the tour before. They look familiar. She doesn't trust them. One lady up front had her wig bitten clean off her head at this exhibit last time, so Cristal reminds everyone to secure their belongings, which includes jewelry and hair and she glances at the woman but the woman doesn't meet her eyes. She tells them how happy Townsend Touristiques is to see returning patrons, they are in for a real treat today since the magnolias are in peak bloom. The entire bus oohs and ahhs, except Bald Spot 'n' Goatee and Reflecting Mirror.

Everybody walks off the bus. Cristal waves to Lexus who is trying to play it cool so she doesn't wave back, which hurts Cristal's feelings but she doesn't stop smiling because she doesn't want Lexus to know it hurt her feelings. She shuts the back door of the bus.

Lexus says what she always says, "Please sit at the assigned seat according to the number you were given when you signed up for the tour. If you do not remember your number, one will be assigned to you after everyone has found their seats." In the back row, Bald Spot 'n' Goatee and Reflecting Mirror are arguing about who is going to sit where. "Sirs," she says, "please sit in your assigned seats."

One of them yells "Where's Townsend!" and the other quickly hits him on the arm.

"Sirs!" she says. They stop arguing but they don't sit. Fine, she thinks, see what happens. "Please buckle your seatbelts. Fold your hands on your lap. Cross your ankles. Once the exhibit begins, please do not reach your hands or feet outside of your seat. Do not touch anything. You have been warned."

The men don't sit. She doesn't force them. She doesn't check anyone's seatbelts. Bone-tired and sick of it, she walks to the bus, but doesn't go in. She leans on the doors and cups her hands around her face to look inside to see Cristal curled up in the driver's seat, covered in Lexus's leather jacket, dozing off. Lexus's heart swallows her entire body. She's got to read the note soon.

Reflecting Mirror holds the tanning mirror up under his face standing under the hot sun, sizzling his nose. Bald Spot 'n' Goatee is looking around for Townsend. "He's on the bus! I bet he's hiding," he says to Reflecting Mirror. "Come with me," he says.

Reflecting Mirror says, "I'm tanning, the sun is in high gear right now."

"The skin on your face is going to melt off your bones sunning like that, at least put some oil on," Bald Spot 'n' Goatee says.

"Go oil yourself you windbag."

"Why, I oughta . . ." Bald Spot 'n' Goatee shakes his fist at him. Right then, thick magnolias release from the sky with head size blossoms. The gleam forces Reflecting Mirror to open his eyes, and he drops the tanning mirror. The magnolia blossoms look dead, and they shrivel as they fall. The crowd whoops and hollers. One woman screams in delight, "Here they come!"

"Hold on!" a man says.

Fifteen magnolia blossoms suspend in the air above them. They come alive, glowing white and green, petals turning like a holy lotus. They grow bigger and bigger until they are the size of a coffin. They float daintily and land at the feet of each person, including Bald Spot 'n' Goatee and Reflecting Mirror. A few women squeal. The magnolias emit gold glitter that covers everyone, and it gets into Bald Spot 'n' Goatee's goatee and makes him sneeze. Willie Earl's laugh emits a highpitched noise from the magnolia that forces the two men to cover their ears with their hands and lean over to examine the flowers more closely.

Before they can ask any questions or say one word, the blossoms shoot into the air, flip themselves over, and chomp down on the heads of Bald Spot 'n' Goatee and Reflecting Mirror, snapping their necks like stalks. The peduncle of each magnolia swallows and sucks like a human throat, Adam's apple traveling up and down, and a little blood leaks from their mouths. The rest of the rich people do not pay attention to what is happening to the men, too delighted in their own experience of being sprayed with glitter and tickled with the tongue and teeth of their own magnolias. When the magnolias are finished and retreat back into the sky, spinning slowly and gloriously, the men's bodies fall silently to the ground, without blood. The magnolias have drunk their fill.

July 26

Once upon a time across the bridge from the broke-ass mildewing casino, Auntie Anita and Uncle Gerald are nestled snug in their beds. Across the street on the third floor, Otis and Leviticus are nestled snug in Otis's bed. Down the hall, Joy and Cora Mae are nestled snug in their beds, lying on their sides while a softly snoring Joy holds Cora Mae in her white nightgown like a teddy bear, their chests rising and falling in sync.

Cora Mae hears her name whispered over and over, and she slips out of Joy's arms, sits up. Joy rolls over, folds her arms into her chest, keeps snoring. Cora Mae crawls out of the bed, walks out of the room, out the apartment door. With her left hand sliding along the banister, she walks her bare feet down one flight of stairs, turns, down another flight, turns again, and down another flight, until she's on the main floor and walking into the street.

Auntie Anita is dreaming Cora Mae gets out of bed in her white nightgown and walks barefoot down the stairs into the street. Dreaming Cora Mae is walking in the middle of the street, even steps, soft steps, toes spreading slightly with each footfall, stepping and stepping toward the bay. Auntie Anita is dreaming she's following Cora Mae, and Auntie Anita is also Cora Mae, seeing what Cora Mae sees and hearing her name whispered over and over: *Cora Mae . . . Cora Mae.*

Auntie Anita following Cora Mae/Anita gets to the edge of the water, one foot into the thick purple, then the other, and keeps walking in until the water is thigh high, nightgown billowing with air until it absorbs the purple up to her waist. Keeps walking until the water is waist-high, chest-high, neck-high, then starts to ascend like walking up steps until she is standing on top of the water. She keeps walking, leaving gentle wakes as her ankles glide through the purple. Her wet, white nightgown clings to her little body. Auntie Anita is in bed pinch-pulling her nightgown away from her body.

Auntie Anita following Cora Mae/Anita continues to walk, and they see the woman in waders standing on the surface in the center of the bay. *Cora Mae . . . Cora Mae*, the sound emits in surround sound, pulling Cora Mae/Anita closer and closer, until they are standing in front of the woman. Her eyes flash with a moving picture of a baby walking on water. Cora Mae/Anita recognize the picture. The baby is Cora Mae. The woman lowers herself into the water. Cora Mae/Anita raises their arms above their head until their fingers touch pointed to the sky. They bring their feet together and point their toes downward. They drop. Whoosh.

The splash makes Auntie Anita shoot up and gasp for air in her bed. She shakes Uncle Gerald: "Get up! Get up! Cora Mae is in the bay! We gotta get Joy!" They don't put on shoes, and rush out the door, across the street, up three flights of stairs, and spill into Joy and Otis's. "Joy! Otis!" Auntie Anita runs down the hall and into Joy's room. "Is Cora Mae in here?"

Joy says, "She's right here," feeling the empty spot next to her. She gets up and pulls the covers back, throws them on the floor.

"She's in the water!" Auntie Anita says.

They all run down the stairs and into the street.

Willie Earl has woken up and is out on his balcony trying to figure out what the hell all the ruckus is about. He sees everyone running in the street shouting "Cora Mae!", so he hops over his banister and follows.

Cora Mae is sinking into the water like a spike, her arms and toes still pointed. A bubble of air surrounds her. Next to her is the woman in waders, her hand reaching inside the bubble to the small of Cora Mae's back, guiding. Both going down down down into the dark. The only light is the woman's flashing eyes. They reach the bottom and Cora Mae's feet billow up a cloud of sand surrounding her and the woman.

Auntie Anita, Joy, and everyone else reach the sandy mud leading to the water to see Cora Mae's small footprints disappear in the purple. Joy dives into the water crying, coming up for air, diving again, nothing. Auntie Anita is running on the water, her ankles leaving violent wakes, her white nightgown clinging to her body. Otis and Joy go to the dock behind the juke joint and hop in a boat, start rowing, trying to catch Auntie Anita.

Once the cloud of sand settles around Cora Mae and the woman in waders, they are standing in the middle of a circle of people dressed in waders like the woman. They are all rooted with sand up to their shins, some look like they are trying to run, some bent over with their arms stuck up to their elbows, some bent over with their arms in plastic buckets full of cockle shells.

Cora Mae, in her air bubble, walks up to each person, their eyes moving side to side and widening inside of their stationary heads. Pleading eyes. There are two more people, a man and a woman, who are lying on their sides, hands covering holes in their chests and ribs. They look at Cora Mae lovingly and she feels a familial warmth growing inside of her. The bubble extends with Cora Mae's arm as she reaches out to touch their foreheads. The bubble extends as she rests her hand on each person's shoulder who is bent over, and on each person's back who is standing. The woman in waders looks pleased, her eyes stop flashing.

Auntie Anita is still running to the spot, to the spot she dreamed that she/Cora Mae sank into the water. She looks around, then downward but sees nothing but purple dark. Joy and Otis are approaching Auntie Anita in the boat: "Auntie!" Auntie Anita feels defeated, thinking that she needs to go down into the water, but can't will herself to. She starts crying. Joy stands and readies herself to dive, and as soon as she bends her knees, they all hear the water bubbling, upward pressure, then the pop of air breaking the surface. Cora Mae rises out of the water next to Auntie Anita. Auntie Anita squats to see if she's okay, but Cora Mae hugs Anita with closed fists and Auntie Anita holds her. Joy and Otis are standing in the boat with their mouths wide. After Cora Mae lets go of the hug, she opens both of her hands toward Auntie Anita: a cockle shell in each hand. She sings Auntie Anita's song softly, "I don't care what they say, sumthin's at the bottom of the bay. You have to go down, Auntie."

They get into the boat with Joy and Otis. Joy hugs Cora Mae, and Cora Mae says, "I love you, Mama. Grandma and Grandpa said they love you." Then she turns to Auntie Anita and says, "The fishery."

July 27

Once upon a time at midnight, on the bay where the bridge piers rise out of the water, Lexus and Cristal are bent over in the arch of the pier shin-deep in the rainbow swirls where the water rejects the tannery oils, and they are trying to collect cockle shells, but having no luck tonight.

Lexus looks over at Cristal and thinks I love her purple lipstick, I love her red hair, I'm going to tell her today how much I love her. As she reaches down into the sand, the cockle shells are smooth and gritty but just as fast as she can grab a hold of one, they disappear.

With every recession of crest, new cockle shells by the moonlight shine gemstone in hue but always soft white with those black laced ridges, and always disappearing again. In the front pocket of Lexus's overalls is the read-me-later note, which she did, read it on the way over to pick up Cristal from Auntie Anita and Uncle Gerald's front porch. Tonight, she noticed the lamp in Auntie Anita and Uncle Gerald's room was off, which it never is. When they interlocked hands to cross the street, she noticed Joy's living room light on through the blinds. She noted to be nosy about it later in the morning.

"I saw you with Whatsername yesterday after our tour shift," Cristal says. "You seeing her or . . ." and she trails off, hunched over and reaching fast into the sand for the shell before the wave hits her legs and she loses it again.

"What's in the distance there?" Lexus thinks she sees the glint of a fish jump.

"You know, that big wily trout Willie Earl and Uncle Gerald are always cussing about with the fisherman," the wind swallowing the last half of what Cristal says.

Lexus wants to say something. She wants to tell Cristal that she was with Whatsername yesterday, but it doesn't matter, because she loves Cristal. The way she looks at her and touches her, shows up for her, the way they kiss, the way their bodies sync and sway and dip into each other perfectly, they are made for each other.

"I think I'm almost tapped out," Cristal says, which Lexus knows she means she's going to want to go home soon.

Give me a sign, Lexus says in her mind to the bridge, as if the bridge will answer, and there, between the slats, she swears she sees Willie Earl's laugh twinkling, can hear the tink over the waves. Cristal slaps the water with her hand and then whispers sorry. Lexus winks at Willie Earl's laugh. Cristal is so kind, she even thinks the water has feelings, which it might for all Lexus knows. This bay is more powerful than anything she can imagine.

"Look," Lexus says. "I need to tell you something." Cristal stands up straight. As she stands, Lexus sees another glint behind her, closer now. Another. Another. Glints coming toward them, steady and fast, with every wave crest, the waves picking up speed as if a boat is ripping through the no-wake zone but there are no boats and the moon shines bright through the purple fog. Lexus says, "We should go," and without hesitation Cristal follows, but her foot gets stuck in the sand as if something below her is grabbing it, she can feel the tendrils as fingers.

Lexus reaches the shore and tries to catch her breath but can't. She starts coughing and wheezing and pounds her chest with her fists to free up the graininess she can feel. Cristal is calling for her but she can't hear her over her own coughs and the waves, now up to Cristal's waist, soaking her T-shirt. Cristal tries to walk forward but she can't, the hand sand won't let her, instead the undertow pulls her back, and right when she thinks she is going to go completely under, the glints circle her, bringing her back up to the surface. There are five, ten, fifteen, twenty, she loses count. Rainbow trout as big as men, as big as Uncle Gerald, as big as Willie Earl, they weren't lying. They crest with the waves as she stands. She moves her feet and the sand recoils, the hand releases her but not before she can feel the overgrown nails scrape her ankle.

Lexus is doubled over on the sand, pounding her chest, pounding the sand with her fists, she can't stop coughing. She thinks, what if this is it, but then a rush of oxygen fills her body and propels her to stand. She runs toward the bay, Cristal falling into her arms. The rainbow trout at the shore open their mouths and sing the song she recognizes as Anita's rapture song, the one she is always singing.

Lexus and Cristal start to dance in the water. The fishes' eyes glaze over as red diamonds, alexandrite, serendibite, emeralds, fire opal, pearls, black hibonite spew out of their mouths, raining gemstones onto the sand. Willie Earl's laugh dances in the gemstone rain. Each fish coughs out one single cockle shell on top of each pile of gemstones before they flop back and return to the water, swishing their way into the dark.

Cristal and Lexus sit on the piles of stones blazing bright in the darkness. Lexus picks up a large red diamond and hands it to Cristal and says, "I love you." Cristal throws the cockle shell from the top of the fire opal pile to the side, and it skips itself all the way across the water until a trout swallows it. She grabs the largest fire opal and hands it to Lexus: "I love you, too." Lexus puts the fire opal in the front pocket of her overalls, and it dissolves the note.

They swear they hear Anita and Gerald, Joy and Cora Mae, Leviticus and Otis, and even Willie Earl cheering somewhere far away.

July 28

Once upon a time down the street from the molded and mildewed casino, Cristal pulls the bus into the parking lot of the police station. She and Lexus keep smiling at each other, mouthing thick I love yous, and feeling full of newness. Lexus stands and runs down the same directions, "Don't worry, we're not putting you all in jail. Our next exhibit, entitled "Le Soirée," is on the old access road behind the police station." Lexus walks up the aisle as usual and gives everyone a faded yellow cone party hat with a black veil attached to the front. Lexus walks back to the front. "Please put on your hat-veil before exiting."

Golden Chalice grimaces beneath his hat-veil. He's looking for the Artist, for Townsend, any sign, any clue, repeating to himself what Lime-Green Velour Robe told him last night "Find Townsend or pay the price with your life."

At the meeting last night, there were only three Owners left: Lime-Green Velour Robe, Birthmark with the Gun, and himself. Lime-Green Velour Robe said, "I'm depending on you, those other imbeciles, I mean traitorous morons, have abandoned our cause. They've flipped and are working for Townsend. No one has seen them, no one," he said slamming his fist on the table. "Traitors!"

When everyone starts to file off the bus, Golden Chalice slides down into his seat so he won't be seen, finishes drinking his whiskey and witch hazel, then stuffs the chalice into the inside pocket of his black blazer. Once everyone is off the bus and huddled around Cristal and Lexus giving further instructions for "Le Soirée," the man slips out and rolls underneath the bus. He peeks up to make sure no one is watching, then rolls out and squat-runs with the veil pressing against his face, headed the opposite direction around the police station to the exhibit. The two phonographs with brass flaring horns are already spinning wobbly records playing a deep voiced static loop of *Lollipop Lollipop*. He ducks underneath the faded and leaning dock, waits.

Rumor has it this is the day the last two caskets will open, or so Lime-Green Velour Robe told him, and the Artist and Townsend will be hiding in the last two caskets. They will remain in the caskets until the next tour, or they will leave and come back to get in the caskets before the next tour. "Either way," Lime-Green Velour Robe said, "This is your chance to kill them both inside the caskets, or follow them to where they hide and kill them there."

Golden Chalice waits as he hears the footsteps, sees through the cracks in the wooden planks, people stopping at:

Casket One: [opened] filled with the purple bay water bubbling. Smiling rubber ducks float and bump into each other.

Casket Two: [opened] filled with the purple bay water surrounding a miniature model of Tannery Bay flooded halfway up to the casino.

Casket Three: [opened] filled with hot purple bay water bubbling and steaming. Casino chips and cockle shells floating. A white sign on the inside that runs the length of the opened lid says: All You Can Eat.

Casket Four: [closed]

Casket Five: [closed]

Golden Chalice is underneath the dock where the last two caskets are. As usual, the people plead to know what's in the caskets. As usual, Lexus tells them to imagine, tells them their worst fears are in there. Golden Chalice is waiting, gripping a pole so he won't fall into the water. The people try to open the caskets but can't. He is thinking this is it, this is it. As usual, the people keep taking turns, teamwork, fingers on every inch of the casket lid prying, grunting and prying and grunting. Nothing.

Golden Chalice hears the people walk off the docks. He's confused.

"What kind of trickery is this?" one of the women says while flinging her party hat-veil over the side into the water, "I thought today was the day the caskets were going to open." Mumbles and groans bellow from everyone. "I wanna see my worst fears," one of the men whines.

Once the bus is driving away, Golden Chalice climbs up onto the docks, his chalice swinging heavy inside of his breast pocket. He tries to open the fifth casket but it doesn't open. He tries the fourth, not moving. He goes to the third casket, intrigued by the All You Can Eat sign and the bubbling water.

Although no one has ever eaten from the casket, he has the idea that maybe drinking from it is the key to getting the caskets open. He feels victorious as he pulls the chalice from his breast pocket, grinning a smart grin, and dips the chalice into the bubbling and steaming purple, filling to the brim. He gestures a little toast, "To you, fucking Townsend," then brings it slowly to his lips, and guzzles. It burns going down, but he keeps drinking, purple oozing from the corners of his mouth, until it's gone. Nothing happens.

His stomach starts gurgling and roiling. He drops the chalice, bends in pain, holding his belly with both arms, trying to clench his anus but the purple shoots out anyway, filling up his underwear first then sliding down his hamstrings.

He stands, groaning, then hears a creak. He whips his head

around and sees the fifth casket opening, so he runs to it and jams his fingers in the crack, lifting with all his might. The casket opens a little more, so he shoves his arms in up to his elbows, feeling around. The casket opens more, and something inside pulls him in while the lid is chomping his upper arms, chomping his head, chomping his back, butt, legs, feet. The casket walks off the edge of the dock and splashes into the bay, drifts down, down, down, and right before it hits the bottom, a rainbow trout swoops up and swallows it whole.

Willie Earl's laugh reverberates from Casket Four.

July 29

Once upon a time at the top of the hills, a button inside the mansion of Lime-Green Velour Robe opens a spring hinge steel door revealing a long hallway with blinking overhead lights, then another spring hinge steel door with a long hallway with blinking overhead lights, and then another spring hinge steel door which leads to a basement chamber under his house.

Birthmark with the Gun always hits his head on the ceiling of the final hallway going left and never expects the door to be around the corner again. He cusses a long string of cuss words. He waits for the door to open, but he gets impatient so he bangs on the door with the handle of the gun. "Come on, you stupid bastard, let me in already, I don't got all day," which is a lie because he does have all day, this is his only task, to kill Townsend. The door opens so slowly, mocking him.

Lime-Green Velour Robe has his feet up on the long executive table, the same table that is in his house. This time, there are only two chairs, one for Birthmark with the Gun and one for him, all the other chairs have been removed. The wall behind him is covered floor to ceiling with maps, blueprints, graphs and tables, photographs, newspaper clippings. When Birthmark with the Gun takes a seat, Lime-Green Velour Robe slams both of his fists onto the wall repeatedly. "Where. Is. Townsend! Where. Are. The. rest. Of. The. Owners!" He points at Birthmark with the Gun and Birthmark points the gun at him. "Tell me right this minute goddamn it! Put that thing away or I'll stick it so far up your ass it'll blow you to smithereens you spineless rat!" Birthmark lowers the gun to the table, but never takes his hand off the trigger. "I ought to slit your throat pointing that shit at me!" he says, as he runs both hands through his hair. He's sweating through his robe, his underarms growing larger and larger circles.

Birthmark with the Gun starts spinning the gun by the trigger on the table. "I saw something yesterday, boss. I think we have competition. When I was out trailing behind the tour bus, a person dressed in a dark cloak was creating sculptures down by the docks, over by the old dusty juke joint. I could see the lights, almost like it was coming from the robe itself."

"So, what of it?" Lime-Green Velour Robe is pacing. He is studying the wall, occasionally scratching his ass, pointing to various things and talking to himself about numbers being down, about all the customer complaints in the past week, doesn't make sense, he grumbles.

"I think it's a new artist, competition for Townsend, or rather us, since Townsend will be dead."

Lime-Green Velour Robe turns around and places both of his hands on the table, leans forward in a power stance. "I swear to god, if you're lying to me, I'm gonna string your nuts on the flagpole of the fucking casino, I swear to god."

"I'm not lying to you, boss, I promise. After I kill Townsend, I'll find the new artist, who's probably not good anyway, but we won't have any competition. We gotta off them all," he says.

Lime-Green Velour Robe is leaning up against the wall with both hands, arms extended. He then starts ripping everything down, rips the maps and the photographs, and the newspaper clippings. With fists stuffed full, he turns around and shakes it at Birthmark with the Gun. "Find them and kill them!" he yells, throwing the fists of garbage at the man.

July 30

Once upon a time on the north side of the casino, William Earl Townsend III and Delores the Artist stand next to a table in the middle of the stage of the amphitheater, waiting for the two remaining Owners to enter. Willie Earl in his pinstriped suit, and Delores in her artist outfit with large black sunglasses. Joy and Uncle Gerald hide on the side like last time, to make sure everything is going as planned. Before they all left the house this morning, Joy told them to do everything as the last meeting: "Keep up the ridiculous-ass, inconvenient show of power," she said. "It keeps them in line and off-balance."

The two Owners walk single file to the entrance. Birthmark with the Gun tucks the gun into the back of his pants while walking behind Lime-Green Velour Robe who is carrying a black leather briefcase handcuffed to his wrist. Lexus greets them at the entrance and says, "Thank you for your silence before entering this sacred space. The Artist does not like frivolous noise. If you feel like you must speak to the Artist and Mr. Townsend, please do so in an orderly fashion, or there will be no meeting, no deals, and you will return to your homes."

Lime-Green Velour Robe says, "We are here to speak and—"

"Quiet!" Lexus says. "Now please, keep walking single file, slowly, until you reach the bottom row of the amphitheater. Once there you will sit next to each other, with your hands in your laps. I must reiterate, any outbursts or sudden movements, and the meeting will be over, OH-VERR."

Once the men sit, William Earl Townsend III says, "Gentlemen. Welcome. I trust you have been informed of the rules for today's meeting. Please take a few minutes to silently designate one person amongst you who will speak for all of you."

Lime-Green Velour Robe raises his hand, "Yes, Mr. Town—I mean, William Earl Townsend III." He pats the briefcase sitting in his lap. "We have a business proposition I'm certain will be lucrative for all involved."

"What do you bring to the table today?" Willie Earl says.

Delores the Artist nods in agreement.

Lime-Green Velour Robe says, "Inside this briefcase is our ledger book. It's a crucial, high-priority document, the key to an even more successful future for you and your client."

"Good for you, on all accounts," Willie Earl says. "You may continue with your proposition."

"May we approach the stage so that we may show you the ledger book while we continue with our proposition."

"Only one of you may approach," Willie Earl says and turns to Delores, "Does this suit you?" She nods.

Lime-Green Velour Robe stands and walks to the stage. He places the briefcase on the table facing Willie Earl and Delores. He removes a key from the pocket of his robe, unlocks the handcuffs and the briefcase. Inside it is a stack of papers and a green canvas book. Delores looks surprised under her sunglasses, thinking, it ain't the same ledger book from the meetings, these muthafuckas think they slick. Willie Earl knows it's a fake because they all know it's a burgundy leather ledger book. Willie Earl picks up the book and holds it to his face so Joy and Gerald can also see it's fake, too, then places it on the table. "Continue with your proposal."

Lime-Green Velour Robe opens the book, running his fingers along ledger lines: "As you can see here, William Earl Townsend

III and Esteemed Artist, going back twenty Julys, we have made considerable profits from the casino and the tannery. Of course we haven't profited from the old fishery because it has been inoperative for a number of Julys. However, it is prime, prime, bayview real estate." He looks up smiling.

"I see," Willie Earl says. "You all have been quite successful, and I applaud your continued efforts. But I do not understand how this is a proposal."

"I'm getting there, sir," Lime-Green Velour Robe says, flipping to the most recent part of the ledger. "What we are proposing, is a trade, your one business, for our three combined businesses. Now you may ask yourself, 'Why are you proposing?' We are proposing because, based on our past successes and our power in this town, we firmly believe we can expand Townsend Touristiques into something exceedingly more profitable for your client, without cutting you out, of course. This is why we are offering you our conglomeration of successful business."

Willie Earl nods, stalls for a minute, because this is their plan as well. "I see," he says.

"Also," Lime-Green Velour Robe says. "If you look here toward the end, you'll see all of our liquid assets are currently allocated for repairs for the unfortunate damages caused by the flooding, as I'm sure you're well aware of. Also why we're offering you full control of all our business henceforth. This does mean the Esteemed Artist will continue to create, for us, that is."

"I think these are somewhat reasonable terms," Willie Earl says, and turns to Delores. "Does this suit you?"

Delores doesn't move, then folds her hands in front of her, then finally nods yes.

Lime-Green Velour Robe says, "Excellent."

"I only want what's best for my client," Willie Earl says. "There is one small detail troubling me. I said 'somewhat reasonable' because the lack of liquid assets concerns me for rebuilding businesses under repair from severe flood damage. With that said, I require something which I can convert to liquid assets if need be . . . I require each of the Owners' homes, as part of a packaged deal along with the aforementioned business properties."

Lime-Green Velour Robe looks a little surprised, but tries not to show it, and does some quick figuring, determines with all the money he'll make from the bus tour, he'd still be able to afford to buy homes anywhere else in Tannery Bay, or even buy back his own home if he wanted, hopefully. He's afraid Townsend will back out if he doesn't offer the homes. "Sounds fine to me, you deserve as much, considering the lack of liquid assets."

"Congratulations," Lime-Green Velour Robe says, reaching out to shake Delores's hand but she doesn't shake it. "And congratulations to you Townsend, you are now the proud owner of Tannery Bay Casino, Tannery Bay Tannery, the *Tannery Bay Daily*, and the old Tannery Bay Fishery."

"Congratulations to you," Willie Earl says. "You are now the owner of the cutting-edge Townsend Touristiques. Perhaps a name change is in order."

Lime-Green Velour Robe motions to Birthmark with the Gun to get up and leave with him. When they're out of the amphitheater, Lime-Green Velour Robe says, "We did it, and we didn't have to kill Townsend. And we did it without those other lowlife traitors. We can split all this money we'll make between us two. Townsend is a fucking fool." They smile at each other even though Birthmark thinks about shooting Lime-Green Velour Robe and stashing his body in that basement of his, and Lime-Green Velour

July 31

Once upon a time across the bridge, past the graveyard and the casino, the tannery, and the fishery that now Willie Earl and Delores own, at the bottom of the hills and up the side of the road, all the rich people are stuck in the mud, their RVs and campers and fancy cars that shouldn't be off-roading to begin with spinning their wheels with no traction. This group has been here all weekend long, waiting for Monday morning when the tour will open again. No one is answering the phones anymore at Townsend Touristiques. No one can get on the list, it's so exclusive, a wife told another wife at the country club playing tennis a few days ago. Everyone has heard the gossip over the weekend about the newest exhibits, the thrill of almost being murdered, the rush is like an orgasm another woman told her book club and while they blushed they wrote down what she said and were jealous. It had become unclear in their circles who was telling the truth and who was lying for prestige. The rumors about what was happening at the exhibits keeps getting more extreme, more dangerous, more fun, and the cost to attend keeps rising, but yes, we will pay, they all say, for the exclusivity of the experience.

Here in the mud, the men tuck in their shirts or roll up their sleeves and try to push the smaller vehicles down and out of the way to make room for the larger ones. The women whimper and stand off to the side, fan themselves with makeshift hand fans made of newspaper with headlines they did not read that say, "Townsend Touristiques Closes Tour." It rained last night for the first time this July, and in their wait for today's art tour they didn't think about getting dirty or stuck or their husbands losing hold of the back bumper and falling flat into the mud, eyeglasses crooked, mad as hell. No one thinks about much of anything these days except to be the first on the latest bus tour. After many men fall into the mud, and many spinning tires, they all decide to leave the vehicles where they are and hike to the first exhibit, the women taking off their high heels and walking barefoot. All uphill, some parts of the road deep mud, up to shins, and some parts dry as if the rain never touched earth, the longer they walk, the more agitated everyone is. They reach the middle landing halfway up, the first exhibit, and the men are yelling at the women and the women cussing at the men. One by one the fussing and chattering and cussing ceases as they look out over the clearing. One woman, who was, a moment ago, calling her husband a good-for-nothing bastard, clings to his side. One man, who a moment ago was threatening divorce, clasps his wife's waist. The only couple who was holding hands the whole time, even through their griping, release. They look out onto the clearing and there is nothing but wildflowers and pine trees as far as they can see, two doe grazing at a small blackberry bush in the distance. The clearing is no longer a clearing. All forest, no chairs, no orange construction cones, no tornado.

They trudge up the hill, around two switchbacks, and down again to the next exhibit spot in silence. Once next to the bay's edge, they all turn their heads collectively as if on cue to find the sound of beeping on the bay, what they think is a barge in the distance. Some of them shield their eyes in order to try to see the flashing red lights that are a normal accompaniment of such sound, but the pink smog of the tannery on the bay clashes with the sun today, making it impossible to see. There, at the bay's edge, no music, no hat-veils, no creaking caskets, no bowls and spoons or soup or hands reaching out. Lapping water, pebble and sand, receding shoreline, dock.

Further down the line at the next exhibit, down the bay's shoreline, through the backend of the forest at the bottom of the hills, back up again a different way, the rich folks are dirty, tired, and steaming mad. One of the men threatens to sue Townsend for his money back, and another man reminds him they, in fact, didn't pay for this tour yet, and the suing man says, "I will sue him for my emotional distress, look at my wife," and his wife has a smear of dirt down the left side of her face, all the way down her blue and white striped dress shirt, down the front of her khakis from where she slipped and fell as they were walking the miles between exhibits. Another man laughs a laugh of knowing, but is actually laughing at the sight of the other man's wife. "We will sue him for everything he's got, bleed him dry, he can't do this to us!" They all start shouting in agreement. Here, where the magnolia blossoms would rise to greet them, the same thing they had been seeing all morning, a whole lot of nothing—undisturbed forest, electricity poles that weren't there before, squirrels enjoying forage.

"How is it even possible?" one woman says.

"Doesn't make any sense at all!" another woman says.

"I want to speak to a manager at once!" another woman says.

All the women agree, yes, they will speak to a manager at once, they will write well-written notes as soon as they get home and get cleaned up. Someone, somewhere, will be hearing from them promptly. They will even call the police.

Where there was one squirrel, now there is a gang of squirrels, more joining every second, jumping from tree branches, popping up from leaf piles, charging the group in droves.

One jumps on one of the women's backs and she screams. Another attacks a man's pant legs and as he tries to kick it off, three more attack his backside. The rest of the squirrels pelt thousands of acorns at them. The rich folks run as fast as they can away from the squirrels and the rain of acorns. One woman yells "This is not art!" snatching a squirrel out of her purse.

They run to the opening of the forest. There is a large wooden sign staked into the ground: Welcome Honored Guests! With Deep Sadness and Regret We Wish You Adieu. Danke and Good Day, Townsend Touristiques.

"I'll be sonuvabitch, we have been swindled!" says a man.

One woman begins to cry and says "I'm so upset! What will I tell my calisthenics class? I can't be the only one who hasn't seen the art yet!"

Another woman comforts her, "It's okay, dear, we will talk to a manager."

One of the men says, "I'll destroy Townsend!" Another man puts his hand on his shoulder and the man who has threatened to destroy Townsend shakes the hand off of him, and looks around hoping no one saw another man comforting him.

Meanwhile, down by the fishery, out by the docks, the beeping is not from a barge. The fishermen in the garden try to ignore the sound but once the noise becomes too loud they worry about the vibration of it hurting their plants, so they lay their trowels down and come out to see. Everyone waves to the truck driver backing up to the side door of the juke joint. The baskets in the fishermen's arms are filled to the brim with vegetables, fruits, flowers, herbs. They take their gardening aprons off and set the baskets down on top, they tighten the locks on the flaps to the garden's entrance.

If you're not from around here, the structure looks like a fishing shanty about to blow over. The truck bed is long and filled sky high, the trailer behind it is covered with tarps, wrapped tight with bungee cords of all colors. Nobody on this side of Tannery Bay has been on the bus tour because, why should they? Auntie Anita makes the best art on this side of town anyway. "What's hidin underneath all this spirit wrap?" a fisherman says and Rashaad hits the back of the trailer with his hand before unhitching it. "Come help me unload if y'all got time, Auntie Anita will be here soon." With the mention of Auntie Anita's name, the fishermen put on their work gloves. One of them unlocks the side door to the juke joint, and props it open with a box full of cockle shells that's been sitting outside. He thinks for a second how he doesn't know where the box came from, how it wasn't there yesterday, or was it? No matter, they got work to do.

Later in the evening, the pink sky streaks like vapor trails, rainbow shimmer gas-on-water glow through the smog hung heavy all day. Auntie Anita sits at the bar while Uncle Gerald serves up a shimmering crystal glass of hooch. Lexus and Cristal are busy behind Auntie Anita unwrapping her sculptures and asking where they should put them, with Auntie Anita finally saying, "Wherever feels good, I'm not god, make it pretty," because she doesn't want to be bothered, the deep low simmer of Etta James in the air, Auntie Anita leaning over to kiss Uncle Gerald on his face while he closes his eyes and sips deep, licking his lips. From the water on the bay, if you look close enough, you can make out the light streaming from the juke joint into the night air. You can make out Auntie Anita's sculptures dancing, the young black woman and her baby, still clutching the lightning rod, the three young children from the neighborhood playing jacks and laughing. You can see the life-size dollhouse right outside the garden, now painted a light blue with a red door, hydrangea bushes and Japanese oak trees lush and thriving outside of it. The caskets are glimmering platinum filled with gemstones. You can see the three-inch pandas in a mound rolling around on each other, balancing on balls, drinking water and eating bamboo from the garden the fishermen gave them. The tornados lightly circle the building, creating a comforting breeze. Through the windows of the juke joint, you can see the line of twenty-four karat gold trees, branches holding strong the apples that are now radiating music. When a large magnolia blossom lays its petals out on top of the bar, it shines pink, healthy gums. And Willie Earl's laugh swims its strong arms across the bay, coming up for air and glinting, winking, backstroking and deep diving, all the way from Bowfin Street.

July 32

Once upon a time, Auntie Anita, Uncle Gerald, Otis, Leviticus, Joy, Cora Mae, Willie Earl, Delores, Cristal, Lexus, Charlene, Merle, and the woman in waders all stand on the access road in front of the old fishery.

The woman in waders was tired of Auntie Anita refusing to go in the fishery, even after all the signs in the old juke joint, even after taking Cora Mae to the bottom of the bay. She went into Auntie Anita's house that morning with Cora Mae, busted up into the bedroom, and they both grabbed Auntie Anita by the hands and pulled her down the steps and into the street. Auntie Anita was yelling, "I ain't going, goddammit!" but her feet were moving, "I ain't going!" Uncle Gerald followed.

Willie Earl was on his balcony laughing to his peppers when he saw them in the street, so he followed, with his laugh hitching a ride on his shoulder, perched and cackling. Otis, Leviticus, and Joy heard Auntie Anita yelling, so they ran down the stairs from their apartment and followed.

Charlene, Cristal, and Lexus were sitting on a bench by the bay looking at the thick pink fog and talking about what they wanted to do now the bus tour is over. Charlene said she wanted to get her own place and maybe Cristal and Lexus could live with her if they wanted. Lexus smiled at Cristal in a see-your-mom-is-trying kind of way. Cristal said she'd think about it. Lexus said she wouldn't want to intrude. They heard Auntie Anita yelling, then saw her and everyone else walking along the path, so they followed too. Up the path, through the graveyard, across the cracked and crumbling bay bridge. Cora Mae and the woman in waders never letting go of Anita's hands.

Delores and Merle were standing and smoking outside of the casino, seeing if they could actually repair it, when they saw everyone crossing the bridge, so they followed.

Here they all stand, in front of the old fishery, where Cora Mae and the woman in waders have finally let go of Anita's hands.

Auntie Anita says, "Okay, okay, since we all own it . . . I guess we gotta go in."

"We?" Joy says. "What do you mean we gotta go in? It's clear ol ghost broad want you to go in, Auntie, only you."

Auntie Anita looks around at everyone, looks at the woman in waders who's shaking her head yes. She looks at Uncle Gerald again. He knows what it means, so he says, "Alright baby, I ain't gonna let you go in there by yourself. I'm partly to blame for Betty Lee and Woodrow's death, they was moving hooch for me."

"Gerald," Auntie Anita says. "We've talked about this for who knows how many Julys, and you gotta stop beating yourself up."

"Then why you still beating yourself up about it?" he says, kissing her on the forehead.

The woman in waders stays and plays patty-cake with Cora Mae while Auntie Anita and Uncle Gerald walk down the wide wooden dock to the fishery, which rises on stilts from the pink fog. There are four busted-out windows at the top floor, and two busted-out windows on each side of the entrance: two large wooden sliding doors big enough for trucks to back in and get loaded with bowfin, rainbow trout, bass, sardines, yellow perch, shortnose sturgeon, and cockles.

Uncle Gerald slides one side of the doors to the right, and Auntie Anita slides the other side to the left. Inside is wide open—the light from the broken windows illuminates the wooden balcony of the second floor that runs the perimeter of the building. Underneath the balcony, hanging on walls, are rusted iron poles and hooks, nets, ropes, and pulleys. Some of the wooden tables on the main floor have stacks of empty sardine tins, never packed. In the middle of the main floor is the stairway which leads to the basement with the hidden floor door where Good Ol Pearl Anne and Auntie Anita used to stash Uncle Gerald's hooch.

They hold hands and walk down into the open hallway leading out onto the other dock where she and Pearl Anne would tie their boat in the middle of the night. There are two rooms on each side of the hall, and purple fog spills in from the bay, carpets the floor. Auntie Anita remembers Pearl Anne saying no one has ever gone into one of the rooms on their right, people had tried knocking it down, sawing, axing through the door, but nothing. At the time, Auntie Anita didn't care because she wanted to get in, stash the hooch, and cut across the bay. "Over here, Gerald," Auntie Anita says nodding to the door on the left. "This is where we used to stash the hooch."

Auntie Anita opens the door and they head inside. She lifts the tattered rug, finds the hidden floor door, pulls it up. It's full of Gerald's hooch, the last shipment Betty Lee and Woodrow dropped off before the cops killed them. Uncle Gerald starts to cry, then Auntie Anita starts to cry.

"This ain't it," she says, hopping down waist-high into the hole with the hooch. "I don't think this is what we're here for, but take it." She starts hefting out the cases of hooch to Uncle Gerald who can't stop crying. "I'm so sorry Betty Lee, I'm so sorry Woodrow, I'm so sorry Anita." Auntie Anita is trying to stop crying so she can focus. "This ain't it, Gerald," she says. "It's the door across the hall."

He bends and helps lift Auntie Anita out of the hole, cases of hooch around their feet as they look across the hall. They walk over and she tells him to open it. "Use them big-ass shoulders." He turns the knob and slams his shoulder into the door. It doesn't move. "Put your back into it," she says. Uncle Gerald squats and slams his shoulder again. "You got it, one more time!" He slams his hip into the door. Nothing. He kicks it. Nothing. She says, "Enough now, don't hurt yourself."

She stares at the door shaking her head, "Probably ain't shit in there anyway." But she feels like she should at least try. She twists the knob. The door creaks open. Uncle Gerald's eyes widen. So do Auntie Anita's.

Inside the room are stacks and stacks of newspaper bundles tied with brown twine, wall-to-wall and floor-to-ceiling. Auntie Anita pulls one of the bundles out into the light of the hallway, and she and Uncle Gerald read together silently.

"Thirty-seven," she says nodding. "The woman had thirty-seven shot glasses on the bar, July thirty-seventh! We been stuck in July since it all went down. These papers never saw the light of day."

"Goddamn," Uncle Gerald says with his fist covering his mouth.

Everyone else stops talking and playing when they see Uncle Gerald and Auntie Anita walking out of the fishery. Uncle Gerald carrying a case of hooch, and Auntie Anita carrying a bundle of newspapers. Once they reach everyone, she hands them each a newspaper and they all read making confused faces, shocked faces, angry faces.

The woman in waders, holding Cora Mae's hand, looks pleased at everyone reading, and finally says, "Thank you."

Joy whips her head up toward the woman and says, "Okay now, you can talk? All you had to do was say something instead of popping up in graveyards and shit, scaring the fuck outta people. Taking my kid in that goddamn bay. You done took this haunting shit too far. I oughta drown your ol ghost ass again. You ol water-logged, raggedy bit—"

"Joy!" Otis says, "stop. What's your name, ghost lady?"

"Morecambe." The woman smiles. "I couldn't talk, Joy. We couldn't move on until people knew what happened to us, and until the Owners didn't control Tannery Bay anymore. It's been 732 Julys, 61 years."

Joy looks up to the sky and touches her fingers together, counting. "Oh shit, means this year is 2029?"

"So thank you, Joy, thank you," the woman says.

"You're welcome, Morecambe," Joy says, smiling. "And thank you, too. We got them greedy-ass Owners good, didn't we? I wish Juice was here to see this!"

Morecambe smiles, and thanks everyone else, thanks Willie Earl for the comfort of his laughs living underwater, and kisses Cora Mae on the forehead. Willie Earl starts laughing and his other laughs trapped in the bay bubble to the surface and pop, joining in. Morecambe waves bye, and starts to walk into the bay, but turns to Anita and says, "You should come, Betty Lee and Woodrow want to see you."

"Oh, before you leave," Otis says. "Did you haunt me in the casino that night because I kicked the gravestone?"

Joys blurts out, "Ain't nobody coming to haunt you, Otis!"

Morecambe laughs. "I came because you had a vision about the dead rising up and taking over. We are the dead, and you all were dead, too, in your own ways."

Auntie Anita and Morecambe walk into the bay, and the purple water turns clear, the pink sky starts to fade into blue.

Joy cups her hand to her mouth and yells, "Who gonna clean up all these goddamn cockle shells!"

They make it out to the spot where Morecambe and Cora Mae descended into the water, and Auntie Anita points her arms upward and toes downward. They sink.

At the bottom, all the people are unstuck, their translucent forms floating toward the surface, even Betty Lee and Woodrow, who hug Anita, and they stay embraced until they reach the surface.

July 33

Once upon a time, the final time, past the grown-in forests of the once-clearings where Auntie Anita's exhibits thrilled and killed, past where the tornadoes ripped off the tops of the trees having since grown back stronger than ever, past the magnolia whose blossoms open and keep opening; now down by the shoreline where the bay laps its rainbow oil softly, and silently, up against the black dirt of the beach, the last two living owners of nothing in Tannery Bay rage at the fact that the exhibits are gone, Townsend Touristiques has closed up shop, and they have lost everything.

Birthmark with the Gun holds his gun to his chest while he and Lime-Green Velour Robe sneak around the shore, the purple oil-water soaking and staining the bottom of the robe. Lime-Green Velour Robe is waving his arms like a chicken, pushing his fists in the air, and the thick purple fog chokes his words so Birthmark with the Gun can't hear him. When Birthmark with the Gun thinks he can see him, he gives him a military salute, the barrel of the gun coming forward flat off his forehead. When he gets closer, Birthmark with the Gun can hear Lime-Green Velour Robe saying "Where the hell are those caskets? Where have all the exhibits gone!"

Earlier this morning, all the rich folks who wanted to speak to a manager, who had every intention of writing a well-written note, the men who did not want comfort especially from other men, all of the people displeased they could not have what they wanted immediately, what they did not pay for, what they were not entitled to, stormed Lime-Green Velour Robe's house since it was announced in the paper the sale of the art bus tour to the Owners in exchange for all of their property and houses. Not only those who weren't able to see the exhibits stormed, but everyone they could get angry enough to follow, even those who had been on the tour so many times.

All of these rich people from the Hills blocked the gate with their vehicles and hopped the fence. They ran the long driveway, up through the sprawling lawn, past the dry elephant fountain, to the looming front door and windows. They used hammers and bats to bash everything in, and chainsaws to cut through. Some of the wives broke the windshields of the man's cars.

They screamed. "You fraud! You coward! You will never work in this town again!"

Inside, as the sound of glass breaking resounded through the house, his wife yelled, "Do something!" but Lime-Green Velour Robe did nothing. He shook his wife off and escaped through the steel doors and blinking hallways deep into the basement. Once down there he called Birthmark with the Gun to rescue him, no meet him at the tannery, no meet him at the fishery. "Hurry!" he screamed into the phone, "We must kill Townsend! I don't care who sees it!"

Here at the bay, the rainbow oil-water edges closer as if to take the men completely. The water gaping, choking, dribbling, choking again. They had to see that the exhibits were gone for themselves, they had to see what the people were so mad about.

At that exact moment, Willie Earl's laugh skips from the horizon like a stone, drop and ripple, growing louder the closer to the men's ears it gets. Lime-Green Velour Robe holds his hands over his ears. "Make it stop! Right now! Make it stop!" he yells at Birthmark with the Gun who points the gun one way and then another, unable to get a handle on the direction the noise is coming from.

"Who's there?" Lime-Green Velour Robe yells in all possible directions, choked by the purple fog.

Willie Earl's laugh takes on every octave. Birthmark with the Gun's ears begin to bleed. The purple fog rises from the water, enveloping them fast.

Willie Earl's laugh says, "You looking for me, muthafuckas?" in what sounds like Townsend's voice.

"Shoot!" Lime-Green Velour Robe says while stomping. "Shoot you fucking buffoon! What are you waiting for!" The fog is so thick he can't see anything.

Birthmark with the Gun haphazardly shoots toward the direction of Townsend's voice. Cockle shells rain down, flooding the shore.

The waves stop.

The fog dissipates.

Lime-Green Velour Robe has been shot in the head, half in the water, half on the shoreline.

Birthmark with the Gun splays three feet away. His birthmark and nose bleeding out onto the sand. Instead of a gun, a pile of cockle shells is next to him.

The hand-sand reaches up and pulls their bodies below.

On Bowfin Street, Willie Earl's laugh swoops down and swirls around everyone outside of Uncle Gerald and Auntie Anita's house, who are not bothered by what happened at the shoreline, but feel the peace that awaits them. Aretha Franklin is blaring onto the street from their front window. Cora Mae is on Uncle Gerald's shoulders dancing around yelling "Happy Birthday! Happy

Birthday!" Otis and Leviticus are hammering a wooden sign together Auntie Anita will paint later that says "Juke Joint: OPEN ('til the end of time)." Joy and Merle are sitting on the hood of her truck laughing and making plans to reopen the casino as a community center.

Cristal and Lexus are singing along, cuddled up on the porch steps with Willie Earl and Delores who are drinking hooch and laughing.

Charlene, walking by dipping and snapping her fingers says, "Y'all won't believe what I just saw down on the bay."

"Lay it on us, Charlene!" Willie Earl says.

"I'll lay something on you, Willie Earl!" Charlene says.

Willie Earl laughs, and his laugh circles around into the air, making Auntie Anita's symbols in rainbow steaks.

Auntie Anita is tipped back in her rocking chair, watching her family and friends, remembering the breeze on the back of the motorcycle going through the Hills, thinking, Gerald and I should get us a motorcycle. She starts humming her rapture song.

PS:
May 3, 2030

Across the clear blue bay from the newly refurbished and reopened Gerald's Juke Joint, the late afternoon sun shines through the new stained glass walls and roof of the old fishery. Every once wooden exterior surface is now stained glass, vibrant colors, designed and built by Auntie Anita and the neighborhood kids and teens who take her art classes. From panel to panel, starting at the entrance, stained glass images tell the story of Morcambe and the rest of the cockle pickers. The roof is made of portraits for each of the thirty-seven cockle pickers with their names underneath. Auntie Anita said it feels holy to look up, and when people come to visit the new fishery they should also be able to feel the holiness, like they are in the best, safest church. Some people notice their own names on the roof, and even recognize their facial features on the people in the panels, and find themselves weeping at the new kinship.

Up the street, the old tannery is the new Rashaad's Repair on one side, and Merle's Plumbing: Getting Your Shit Together on the other side. Charlene stayed on as secretary, and Otis came on as partner plumber. Cristal is Rashaad's partner mechanic.

Up the street, the no longer dilapidated, mildewed, and broke-ass casino is the new T-Bay Community Center where Auntie Anita holds her art classes. Joy teaches events coordination and leadership. Willie Earl teaches food preservation and preparation (with a specialty of his hot sauce and pickled peppers) and horticulture in the newly added greenhouse. Delores, Lexus and the rest of the Queers on Gears added a warehouse as the central hub to store and deliver food.

Across the no longer cracked and crumbling bay bridge, Harold & Hattie's Haberdashery is still Harold & Hattie's Haberdashery, but busier, because everyone wants some custom-made threads these days. They wanna be as sharp as William Earl Townsend III. Leviticus has been doing his best to keep up with orders while creating new designs.

Here we are in the golden light of late afternoon, over at the newly refurbished and reopened Gerald's Juke Joint. The entire squad and the neighborhood kids and their parents are gathered for Cora Mae's birthday party. She's five years old. This is her first birthday not measured by or in July. She's sitting, legs dangling over the bar. The new bar is encrusted with red diamonds, alexandrite, serendibite, emeralds, fire opal, pearls, black hibonite, and cockle shells. Cora Mae is wearing a white dress Hattie designed and Harold and Leviticus sewed: one shoulder strap with ruffles cascading diagonally from her chest to her knees.

Uncle Gerald, Cristal, and Charlene are behind the bar pouring hooch for whoever asks for a little nip. Uncle Gerald's eyes are moist because the way Charlene and Cristal flip glasses, and level their heads with the glass while dipping the bottle down then up, is exactly the way Good Ol Pearl Anne poured drinks. Uncle Gerald and Charlene put a red diamond, a fire opal, and a pearl (in honor of Good Ol Pearl Anne) in the bottom of each glass. On the wall behind the bar is a new mural of Mildred and Betty Lee singing, and Woodrow playing drums. Rashaad and Willie Earl sit at the bar telling Cora Mae jokes. Rashaad tells Cora Mae, ". . . and the diamond said, 'don't take me for granite!'" Cora Mae cracks up even though she doesn't get it, she's laughing at Rashaad's enthusiasm, Uncle Gerald doubled over and stomping his foot punctuating his laugh, and Willie Earl slapping his knee with his head back crying. Willie Earl slaps Rashaad on the back and says, "Oh, reminds me." He walks behind the bar, bends, and hefts a canvas sack over the bar. "Here you go, Rashaad! For everything you helped us out with." Rashaad opens the canvas sack and gemstones beam rainbows into his grinning face. He says, "Alright now! Thank you, but I already got a new shop. Imma go on right ahead and give these stones to the community center."

Joy, Merle, and Delores come in the juke joint followed by the breeze of Auntie Anita's tornado. They are carrying a wooden slab with a cake the diameter of a car tire, three tiers of white ruffled frosting to match Cora Mae's dress. They sit the cake on the bar next to her.

Morecambe twirls with Willie Earl's laugh next to Auntie Anita in center stage, shaking her hips to the groove. Lexus is behind her playing piano while nodding at Leviticus on standup bass, who nods back. Otis is finally using his dad's old drumsticks that he kept in his top dresser drawer. He nods at Auntie Anita and she gives him a thumbs up approval to start rolling on the snare to get everyone's attention. Once everyone quiets down, Auntie Anita says, "It's good to see everyone's lovely faces this afternoon, you all are so beautiful, SO beautiful. Thank y'all for coming out to celebrate my baby, my morning dew on grass, the sunlight of my life, my wind that whispers at night, Cora Mae. Alright y'all sing from your gut, on the count of three, one . . . two . . . three!" And everyone sings Happy Birthday Dear Cora Mae as loud as they can.

Once the song is over, Otis walks over and hugs Joy and says, "I love you." Then he hugs Core Mae, and once he releases, he looks her in the eyes and says, "Happy Birthday, Cora Mae, I'm so glad you were born."

Willie Earl's laugh rises to the ceiling and engulfs the juke joint, bursts through the roof to the sky where it takes over the entire bay, where it can be heard from miles and miles around.

Behind the juke joint, Uncle Gerald and Auntie Anita sit on the dock holding hands and swinging their feet, saying hello to the thick morning fog. When the fog lifts, they see a large white cruise ship looming at the entrance of the bay.

No one in Tannery Bay knows this cruise ship is pulling in. No one in Tannery Bay has given this cruise ship permission to pull in. On the ship, the PA system crackles on, and a man's voice statics until clear, "Good morning, passengers. We have arrived at our destination, the mythical Tannery Bay. Our country's personal Atlantis, if you will, disappearing from maps over sixty years ago in 1968. Even modern GPS was unsuccessful at locating the lost town, until it suddenly reappeared with no explanation. But alas, we are here . . ." People in the cabins roll up their beach towels, apply sunscreen, and put on large floppy straw hats. A documentary crew checks and rechecks their equipment. A Time-Share Executive prepares his laptop and steno pad. Superstore location scouts prepare their notes.

Back on the dock, Uncle Gerald and Auntie Anita exchange knowing glances, as Uncle Gerald hits the water, splashing a big splash toward the boat. He says, "It's only been six months. And here they come already!" Auntie Anita shakes her head like it's a shame, balls her free hand into a fist. "I can't believe it! Let's go tell Joy!"

Notes & Acknowledgements

Tannery Bay is based loosely on the cockling disaster that took place in Morecambe Bay, UK in 2004. For the sake of paying homage, the character Morecambe also derives her name from the town of Morecambe Bay.

Auntie Anita's character was inspired by Anita Baker.
Uncle Gerald's character was inspired by Gerald Levert.

Original newspapers images created by Angel Whisenant.

The photograph of the bus is borrowed from *Unsplash* by artist Sangga Rima Roman Selia.

The cover photo is borrowed from *Upslash* by artist Jon Flobrant (@jonflobrant). All dream sequences are inspired by Mathias Svalina, the master dream delivery person. (Find dream delivery at dreamdeliveryservice.com).

Thank you to Jada Dunn for the author photo.

The line, "Ain't nobody coming to haunt you, Otis!" is borrowed from *The Temptations* (TV miniseries, 1998, directed by Allan Arkush) when the actor Leon's character David Ruffin says, "Ain't nobody coming to see you, Otis!"

Credit to The Chordettes's "Lollipop;" All other song lyrics are original to the authors.

Thank you so damn much to our writing group for their years of editing and encouragement for this book: Alex Benke, Alexandra Jackson, Brian Lupo, D. L. Cordero, Joe Ponce, Suzi Q. Smith, and Thuyanh Astbury.

Thank you to Vincent James and *Denver Quarterly*, where an excerpt of this work first appeared in a radically different form.

Thank you to Joanna Ruocco, Sarah Blackman, Dan Waterman, and all of FC2/University of Alabama Press. Thank you for the generous blurbs Kali Fajardo-Anstine, Suzi Q. Smith, and Elle Nash.

Katie Jean: Thank you forever to PJ Carlisle, without whom my writing life would not exist. Steven: Thank you to my wife Tara for everything that allows me to write, and thank you to my kids Jada and Ever for being the shit and inspiring my imagination.